CW00840033

BLACK - SKINNED SCIENTIST AND OTHER STORIES

BARNABA M. ZINGANI

ISBN - 13: 978 - 1537675176
ISBN - 10: 1537675176

DEDICATION

This book is dedicated to my lovely children: Lisungu, Akuzike, Mayamiko and Barnaba Jnr.

Published by Atutulutu Publications
P.O. Box 30290,
Chichiri,
Blantyre 3.
Malawi.
Central Africa.
E - Mail: bzingani@yahoo.com

First Edition 2016

CONTENTS

PREFACE

One thing that made my childhood enjoyable was story telling by my mother, father and grandmother. In those days, there were no televisions. The only entertainment available was radio, gramophone and radiogram. Since I was young, I was not allowed to operate any of them.

When night fell, if the weather was cold, we sat around fire to warm our bodies. The elderly people narrated nice and educative stories one after another, while light from the moon, spiced the occasions. How they kept all those stories in their heads made us appreciate their wisdom. After entertaining us with the stories, they made sure they find out what lessons we had learnt. Each one of us took turns to explain.

The story telling episode stimulated the interest of story telling in us. When the elders were not around, we reminded ourselves the stories they narrated. When one forgot, we reminded each other. One interesting thing was that we imitated how the elders conducted themselves when they narrated the stories. We imitated the mannerisms and laughed.

I have written this book for my children: Lisungu, Akuzike, Mayamiko and Barnaba Jnr. I just wanted to simplify life for them. Instead of them telling their children stories, they would hand over this book to them to read. While my grandchildren will enjoy reading my stories, others would also benefit from it. Any information not documented is lost information. Stories not documented are lost stories. It is like treasure hidden under the earth.

I have no doubt; even elderly people will enjoy reading the stories in this book. Let them stimulate a writing culture in those who at one point listened to stories but never took time to put them down on paper.

ACKNOWLEDGEMENTS

One's success does not stand in isolation. It is supported by other people. When things work out for you, there are people in the background who made their contributions for the intended goal to be achieved. For one to write one needs energy. The type of food one eats, determines the functionality of the brain.

My dear wife made sure that my health is being taken care of. She provided me with nutritious food. I needed time to relax. My children cheered me up. I would not be doing myself justice by not recognising their contributions to my creativity. I, therefore, express my profound gratitude to Agatha, my dear wife and my lovely children: Lisungu, Akuzike, Mayamiko, and Barnaba Jnr for the health breaks. You are so precious. Remain blessed!

No man is an island. My thanks also go to:-

Pascal J. Kishindo, Professor of African Languages and Linguistics, currently the Director of Centre for Language Studies at the University of Malawi - Editing.

Richard Mwale - Layout.

Ralph Mawera - Cover illustrations.

Amanda Nazombe - Translation.

Annie Chimombo - Typing.

Pamella Chiyembekezo - Encouragement.

May the good Lord richly bless you all!

Barnaba M. Zingani.

1

BLACK - SKINNED SCIENTIST

Gani village was famous for witchcraft. Instead of enjoying their sleep, people were busy practicing sorcery. Those who loved night outings met and experienced horrible things. Some met astonishingly very tall people. Others met very short people. Trains were spotted speeding up in maize fields. Surprisingly, no railway line existed. Come morning, the maize plants were still intact in the field.

The village had scientists who only practiced their science at night. Laboratories and workshops for their experiments and engineering activities respectively, were invisible. The village had no electricity, but at night, the graveyard would light up as though it had electricity.

Wise villagers were surprised why the village remained without electricity yet the graveyard was well lit. They couldn't understand the logic of electrifying the graveyard instead of the whole village. White - skinned scientists practiced their witchcraft both at night and during daytime. They generated electricity in the open. Their discoveries had simplified life and made it more enjoyable.

Children were born and grew old. Stories spread that the village had some skilled engineers who manufactured cars, buses, aeroplanes and generated electricity. The challenge was, those skills only became manifested at night. The shameful part of it was that the skills were practiced naked. Why it was so, nobody knew. The connection between the skills and nakedness remained a mystery.

For instance, if the aeroplane manufacturing skill was showcased during daytime; this village could have been the wealthiest on the globe. But it remained the poorest. It had the highest number of school drop - outs. It bred house boys, maids, casual labourers, cleaners, messengers and garden boys for cities and towns. Under aged marriages was the order of the day.

The village had no piped water system. It had no boreholes either. It depended on wells which were dug manually. Livestock and human beings drank water from the same spot. It was a health hazard. Water borne diseases were very common. No year passed without a cholera epidemic. Health surveillance assistants were deployed to control the epidemic. They conducted awareness campaigns. The high illiteracy rate contributed to the failure to eliminate the epidemic.

The villagers were ignorant of flush toilets. When they got admitted to a hospital with running water, they were seen roaming around in search of pit - latrines. In the process, some of them relieved themselves behind the wards. Others opted for the hospital orchard, leaving it so filthy.

The health personnel conducted civic education to those not familiar with flush toilets. The exercise never achieved its intended purpose. The patients drank water from the toilets. They took it to be a well. Furthermore, they were not comfortable to seat on toilet pans. They instead opted to squat. The size of the seat pan never accommodated the squatting. It was, therefore, left with dirt from the feet. Dry and fresh excrement filled the pan, leaving the room with a very strong foul smell.

When the hospital had water problems, patients still frequented the flush toilets. The seat pans became eyesores. If a door to the toilets was left open, a strong foul smell filled the whole ward. Cleaners had tough time. Cleaning was a health hazard. Sometimes, cleaning materials were not available. They had no protective wear. It was a nightmare to keep the toilets clean.

Squatting on the seat pans led to the cistern, a tank that stored water for flushing, fall off the wall. Patients held it to support themselves as they squatted. Some patients fell off. They broke their legs. Fear gripped their minds. They stopped visiting the toilets. When that happened, the casualty was the hospital orchard. Others opted to relieve themselves on the toilet floor.

The hospital placed toilet papers in all toilets for cleaning. The patients were very uncomfortable to use them. They complained that they were too soft. They, therefore, removed the toilet paper rim and used it. They went ahead to use stones, maize - cobs, newspapers, fresh tree leaves, worn out cartons and worn out clothes. The end result was, serious sewer blockages.

Most houses in the village were constructed from mud. They had thatched roofs. Walls and roofs for pit - latrines, were constructed from wooded poles and grass. Bathing rooms had thatched walls. They had no roof. When it rained, no water was required for bathing. They entered the bathrooms with a bathing - soap only. But the problem came when rain stopped abruptly and the head and face were covered by soapsuds.

It was rumoured that Gani village scientists, manufactured their aeroplanes from bamboo; a tropical giant woody grass locally found. The manufacturing period for one aircraft was two weeks. The machines flew at supersonic speeds. Flights were only at night. All road junctions in the village acted as airports.

Two or three ways road junctions were for local flights. Four ways road junction was the international airport. No runways existed. Flight schedule was every night. The pilot would either be a man or a woman. The youth were trained to fly local aircrafts. They were not allowed to fly abroad.

One calm and clear morning, a tragedy befell the village. A boy aged ten, fell off from a witchcraft aircraft. The machine had a mechanical fault. It landed at Mizimu International Airport. The accident occurred just as they were about to land. The boy had a fracture on his left leg. He was admitted to Bweya Hospital. Medical Assistant Joze, wanted to take the history of his sickness.

"What is your name?" he asked.

"My name is Pulu Dzuwu."

"What are you suffering from?"

"I have a fracture on my left leg."

"What was the cause of the fracture?"

"I fell off from a witchcraft aircraft."

Joze was frightened. His writing material dropped to the ground. He bent down. He picked it. He cleaned it with his white dust coat. He stared at the boy for a moment. He coughed to clear his throat since he had flu.

"You are not serious!" Joze exclaimed with amazement.

"I am serious. Are you not aware these aircrafts exist?"

"No, I am not aware. As a matter of fact, I don't believe in witchcraft."

"This night visit me. I will fly you to New York."

"Which New York are you talking about?"

"The famous New York you know."

"You are not serious!"

"I am serious."

"You mean to say, you have been to America?"

"Yes."

"How many times?"

"I have visited New York countless times. Visit me this evening. You will prove me right."

"But why are you dressed up in rags?"

"Don't bother me with so many questions, just visit me this evening."

5

In the evening, Joze visited Pulu in the side ward. The room had two beds. One bed stood next to the window. The other one stood on the opposite side. The beds were well made with blue linen. The colour of linen depended on the ruling party. Two visitors' chairs faced the window. The patient lay on the bed next to the window. Both beds had white painted mobile, side bed lockers.

Ironically, the patient instructed the Medical Assistant to switch off the lights. He switched them off. In a twinkle of an eye, Pulu's body was transformed. He came out of his body. The original body, from which he came out, remained static. He had long fingers and toes. His lips almost grazed the floor. His eyes glowed as though they were torches. The size and length of his ears increased.

He slid his right hand into his pair of trousers' pocket. He pulled out a black plastic bottle. It contained dark watery stuff. He shook it four times. After that, he sprinkled it onto the Medical Assistant's face. Instantly, he transformed. He also came out of his body. His original body, from which he came out, remained static. His fingers, toes, lips, eyes and ears resembled those of Pulu.

"Attention! we are now about to take off. Close your eyes for two seconds and open," Pulu instructed the Medical Assistant. He closed his eyes. Within two seconds, they were in New York.

"Wow! Where are we?"

"You are in New York,"

The Medical Assistant was amazed. He was shown the Statue of Liberty, the Empire State Building, the Central Park, the United Nations Headquarters, the Wall Street and the Fifth Avenue.

"You mean to say, we are in America?"

"Yes my dear, can you close and open your eyes again?" The Medical Assistant followed the instructions. Within two seconds, they were back in the ward. He was so terrified. He came out of the ward. He ran away.

The other team of black - skinned scientists, concentrated on creation. It was made up two groups. One group comprised men and women. They were of different age groups. They created living creatures like crocodiles, hyenas, snakes, rats, goats, cows and birds of different types. These living creatures were not created with good intentions. Crocodiles were created to kill those deemed as enemies.

A huge crocodile would come out of a well and kill a targeted woman who came to draw water. Surprisingly, the size and depth of the well could not accommodate such a huge crocodile. But that was what happened. Such crocodiles flooded even big rivers. They killed targeted victims who came to swim and draw water.

The hyenas, rats and snakes were used for theft. Hyenas were sent to steal cattle and goats. The stolen cattle and goats were handed over to the concerned groups. Rats and snakes stole money from homes and markets. During market days, rats and snakes were seen moving about aimlessly. When attempts to kill them were made, they disappeared.

The other creation group, created lightening. Unlike the first group, it was dominated by elderly people. Most of them had grey hair. The motive behind the creation of lightening was to kill people. It struck people when there was no rain. When rain fell, the situation became worse. More people were struck and killed instantly. Infact, the killers, targeted their own relatives. The benefits for the killings were not clear.

Those who created lightening never enjoyed their trade. The suspects were brutally murdered since they provoked the wrath of people. The sad part of it was, there was no proof. Nobody came in the open to testify that he or she indeed created lightening. The suspects who were mostly elderly people were murdered by their own relatives.

When a youth was killed by a man - made lightening, they teamed up. They murdered the suspects in broad day light. Ageing, therefore, became a scary thing. The older one became the more dangerous life became. Elderly people lived in fear. The number of suspects' - brutally killed, increased with time. Fearing for their lives, the elderly hid in Diso forest where they were devoured by wild animals.

Those who had the skill of creating lightening also created rain. Gifted as they were, they couldn't eliminate droughts. They had a rare skill, worthy exporting abroad. The industry could have promoted their livelihood. These were expatriates playing hide and seek. They could be sent to countries experiencing droughts to arrest them. They could also be invited to turn deserts into estates where assorted crops could be grown. The science that could have transformed peoples' lives was hidden somewhere.

At least those scientists not pursuing the creation of lightening had tangible things to show. Rumours had it that they operated businesses like buses, minibuses, butcheries, supermarkets and pubs. Some built dwelling houses while others owned huge shops and rented them out in cities and towns. They had bank accounts. Of course, how the wealth was accumulated remained a mystery. Nobody came in the open to declare that he was in this industry.

White - skinned scientists manufactured cars, buses, aeroplanes and trains but never practiced the creation of living creatures. Black -

skinned scientists would have an upper hand in that industry. They could have been sole exporters of beef and the like. They would have no competitors on the market, that is if only they came in the open.

Black - skinned scientists could have dominated the market abroad. Imagine the period a cow takes to grow and someone just creates it within seconds! European markets would have been flooded with beef from this village. Man - created cows looked exactly like the God - created cows. The taste of beef for the two cows was not different.

The funniest thing about the black - skinned scientists who claimed to manufacture cars, aeroplanes, buses and trains was, they travelled long distances on foot during the day. They had cracked feet. They dressed so poorly. They wore rags.

The black - skinned scientists couldn't afford shoes let alone slippers, yet they were billionaires at night, shame! During daytime, they were seen having their slippers mended at a shoe repair shop. The question remained, if they really flew on aeroplanes at night, why couldn't they do the same during the day?

One other interesting factor was that the black - skinned scientists in the manufacturing industry together with their children were malnourished. They couldn't support their families financially. At times, they slept on empty stomachs. They watched their government struggle to eliminate poverty.

A combination of scientists in the manufacturing and creation industries was a good reason enough for the village to be exporting electricity, cars and buses abroad. Monies realised from the exports could have been used to boast the economy of their country.

Talented scientists watched people die of hunger. Their existence could have made hunger a story of the past. They could have contributed to the country's foreign reserves. The Kwacha could have been at par with the pound. But alas! during daytime, they cued for food at Farmers' Market depots. Crazy!

Plans to link black - skinned scientist and white - skinned scientist proved futile. They had one thing in common: Both were scientists. But their operations were different. One operated both during the day and night, the other operated only at night.

To make matters worse, it was very difficult to identify the black - skinned scientists. Infact, they didn't want to be identified. They never came into the open. They were so secretive. The white - skinned scientists were open. The machines they manufactured were all over making life easy to manage. Black - skinned scientists benefitted from white skinned - scientists. Their wives cued at grinding mills to have their maize ground.

Were the two teams to be brought together, communication between them would be a problem. Most black - skinned scientists were illiterate. They couldn't speak English. They only spoke their native languages. Interpreters would, therefore, be needed to facilitate communication.

The white - skinned scientists only spoke English. They couldn't speak the black - skinned scientists languages. They had manuals and photographs for their products. The black - skinned scientists had no manuals and no photographs. They never documented anything. If a picture of their night activities was taken and developed, nothing appeared on the photograph. Trying to bring the two together was like trying to bring together North and South Poles.

One blue sky evening, Tobi and his colleagues had a business trip to Kampepuza. The following morning was a market day. They were in the business of second hand clothes. They put on warm clothes in preparation for the cool evening. They stood at Duwa bus stage.

On this day, buses were very scarce. There was no bus that came by. Why buses were scarce was beyond their comprehension. The warm weather gave way to the cool weather. They repeatedly sat down and stood up. They did that to promote a good circulation of blood in their bodies. They had been sitting down for so long. Some jogged a short distance and came back. Others just watched.

The sun went down. Night began to fall. Since they had attached great importance to their journey, they waited for the bus until late in the night. At a distance, they saw a flash of lights. Those who sat stood up. Little by little, the lights approached the stage. In no time, the bus stopped. Their hearts were filled with joy. They sang joyful songs. One by one they boarded the bus. When everybody got in, the bus took off.

On the way, however, peoples' minds were gripped with fear and shock. They discovered that the driver was naked. They were dismayed. They turned to the bus conductor. He had also put on a birthday suit. They were mystified. They trembled with fear. They all sighed, "Ah! what's happening and where are we?"

"Good evening ladies and gentlemen," the conductor greeted the passengers.

"Good evening, Sir," the passengers replied in unison.

"You are most welcome to NDC Bus Services," the conductor

welcomed them with a deep voice.

"What does the abbreviation NDC stand for?" Deya one of the passengers inquired.

"It stands for Naked Driver and Conductor (NDC)," the naked driver chipped in.

"Are you not ashamed of your nakedness?" Tobi, Deya's friend asked boldly.

"You are also naked only that your clothes have covered your nakedness," the driver replied smilingly.

He turned to the passengers. To their surprise, his nose was positioned on his mouth and vice versa. The passengers were confused. They turned to the conductor who by then approached them for payment. He had chameleon eyes. He kept murmuring to himself.

One of the conductor's ears was located on the nose's position, while the nose was located on the ear's position. The other passengers they found in the bus also had abnormal features. Some had one eye on the forehead while others, legs and hands were substituted for each other. The legs were located on the hands position and vice versa.

All the passengers they met in the bus spoke unfamiliar languages. They spoke at the top of their voices. Those with substituted legs and hands had big round heads with sparse long hair. They produced a very strong foul odour that caused the other passengers to sneeze, cough and vomit continuously. Those with one eye on the forehead never blinked.

By and by, as the new passengers tried to figure out what to do, they realised that they were at the same Duwa bus stage they had been waiting for transport. The most bizarre thing happened, all their clothes were torn on the backsides. Trousers and dresses were completely torn leaving their buttocks exposed. For those who stood up, the soles of their shoes were worn out.

"What happened?" Tobi asked with shock.

"I don't know," Deya replied.

"Maybe we took a sorcerer's bus."

"Ah, but then it looked like the buses we ride during daytime."

"That is how a sorcerer's bus looks like. It looks like all other ordinary buses."

"Then why don't they ply their trade during daytime?"

"How can they ply their trade during the daytime in their birthday suits?"

"You are quite right."

In fear of being fooled again, they started off for their homes. They walked together and discussed their ordeal. Amongst them was a one - eyed man. He could have been in his early fifties. He was short. He had a white beard. He explained to them that this witchcraft bus was his second encounter.

"We should count ourselves lucky by returning to Duwa bus stage," the one - eyed man explained calmly.

"Why lucky?" Tobi inquired.

"The first time I encountered this ordeal, we ended up being dumped at a graveyard," he explained.

"Gosh! and what happened next?"

"Each one of us was found lying comfortably on a tomb. While there, we received heavy slaps that sent us back to the bus stage."

"What do they benefit from the mockery?" Deya asked.

"They don't benefit anything. When day falls, they look so miserable."

"Besides, why deprive yourself of a nice sleep and come to mock other people?"

"The time they waste, could have been invested on something productive."

"Did you notice the face of NDC Bus Services driver?"

"Yes, I did, I almost burst out with laughter but I feared he could have swallowed me alive."

An owl was having a nice time on one of the branches of a fig - tree. The tree was located on the eastern side of the road. Tobi commented, "I understand owls are used as weapons of destruction by witches."

"What else would you expect from an ugly creature like that one apart from destruction?"

"Is it the ugliness that makes it a weapon of destruction by witches?"

"I don't know."

"I hope you still remember how ugly the owners of NDC Bus Services were?"

Deya burst out with laughter. He commented, "I never thought you would remember the name of that bus service."

"I couldn't forget it. I didn't enjoy that experience. It is impolite to leave an elderly person like me with bare buttocks. We thought we had taken our seats in that bus yet we were seated on the floor and they took their turns at dragging us." The whole team laughed

11

uncontrollably.

Gani village's graveyard was located at the centre of the village. The team that had been duped by the sorcerer's bus approached it. They were all startled. It glowed as though it had electricity. Trees and tombs could be viewed. Tombs constructed from terrazzo, glittered. Strong whistling and strange songs of owls were heard. Sounds of sneezing and coughing were heard simultaneously.

"What is this now?" Tobi asked with both hands holding his waist.

"I am also astonished. When did Powergen supply electricity to our graveyard?" Deya asked uncomprehendingly.

The one - eyed man replied, "That is black - skinned scientist's electricity."

They all laughed.

"Do you want to view what is happening at the graveyard?" the one - eyed man asked.

"Yes," they all replied.

The man knelt down. He coughed to clear his throat. He turned side ways. He blew his nose. He plucked off a fresh leaf from a shrub. He cleaned the passage of his nose. He took out a small bottle from his bag. It contained water. He opened it. He poured the water on the palm of his right hand. One by one, he rubbed it on their faces. As soon as water was administered, their eyes were opened.

The activities at the graveyard could now be seen. There was a group of naked people, male and female. Their ages ranged from about five to hundred. They had very long lips, almost grazing the ground. They also had very long fingers and toes. They were dancing around the tombs. In their hands, they carried things which resembled the head, hand, leg and intestines of human beings.

"Hey, that man with a big belly, isn't that Tsotsi?" Tobi asked as he shivered like a person with a fever.

"Yes, it's him," the one - eyed man replied.

"And what is he doing?"

"He is creating wealth. All the wealth he has, this is how he creates it."

"Huh, so when we admire wealth; we are actually admiring troubles, eh?"

"True, the sorcerer's bus that we rode on earlier; the naked driver was him."

"Does it mean that all the people who have wealth do this?" Tobi asked.

"No, not everyone, there are some who acquire their wealth in honest ways, but as for these people, this is how they acquire it."

Tobi and his colleagues continued with their journey. They left Tsotsi and his friends at their rituals. The one - eyed man warned his friends about the dangers of passing by graveyards at night. He entertained them with a story of a tall, beautiful half - caste girl, who causes accidents at 18 Area roundabout cemetery at night in Lee - Long - Way.

"Elton, my cousin, was passing by 18 Area roundabout cemetery in his Toyota Fortuner. The night was extremely dark and calm, as if it would rain heavily. A tall, beautiful half - caste girl waved her hand signalling him to stop. He stopped. She opened the door. She went in. She closed the door. She fastened her seat belt. The girl was wearing a white mini skirt. It had a slit that exposed her thighs. She pulled it down below her knees but it couldn't go farther than that. It glittered and changed colour from white to orange. He greeted her. She didn't respond. She kept on peeping through the door window. Once in a while, she turned to him and smiled. He was scared. As he was contemplating to stop the car, the girl disappeared," the one - eyed man explained the ordeal.

"You said she just disappeared?" Deya asked.

"Yes, she vanished into thin air."

"What happened thereafter?"

"Elton lost control. His car swerved. Instead of placing his foot onto the foot break to stop, he placed it on the accelerator. Immediately, the car flew in the air. It hit a street light pole on the right hand side of the road. A heavy bang was heard. Street lights went off. The following morning, he lay flat on a bed in the Male Ward at Kamizu Central Hospital. He had lost his memory. He couldn't recall anything."

"That was too bad!" Tobi exclaimed.

Elton's ordeal, narrated by Juju, the one - eyed man, made their journey short. They were tired and exhausted. "Give my regards to the NDC Bus Services conductor in the morning," Tobi joked with Deya, his friend, as they parted for their respective homes. One thing they never forgot was the NDC Bus Service experience. It was quite an experience worthy encountering in one's life time.

In the morning, Tsotsi walked around with his head bowed. When he met the people whom he had shamefully treated the previous night, he shied away. He had no peace of mind. His reputation began to tarnish. Even though this was the case, he continued to practice witchcraft. He would transform into a hyena and steal from other people's kraal. He stole goats, cows, sheep and other such animals. He had became a very wealthy person.

He had a young man who worked for him. He was close to his heart. His name was Faya. The reason why he cared so much about the boy was that, at a certain time when he fell ill and almost died; he cured him by using herbal medicine. From that point onwards, the two cared a lot for each other.

"Faya my boy, you who is close to my heart, I have decided to reveal to you the secret to my wealth today," Tsotsi started off as he chewed some roots.

"So your wealth has a secret?" Faya asked with a surprise.

"Yes, it has."

He pulled out a small brown stick and a white handkerchief from his pocket, "When I put this stick on the ground and jump over it, I transform into a hyena. After that, I go into people's kraals. I steal different types of livestock. I tie them in a white handkerchief. When I return to the place where I placed the stick, I jump over it and turn back into a human being. I untie the white handkerchief and release the livestock in my kraals."

"How many goats do you tie in one handkerchief?" Faya inquired.

"I tie as many as one hundred."

"Do you tie cows as well?"

"Yes, I do."

"How many?"

"Fifty."

"Fifty?"

"Yes."

"Why don't you start a transportation business?"

"To be transporting what?"

"To be transporting goods. You can make a lot of money. If you are able to carry fifty cows in a handkerchief it means you can transport a container with assorted goods."

"Hahaha!"

"What's funny?"

"What makes me laugh is that most of the things we sorcerers do don't benefit us anything. We enter peoples' houses without breaking the houses but cannot take out even a penny."

"That baffles me as well. If you can enter a house without breaking it, why not enter the banks and collect huge sums of money, wrap them in your magic white handkerchief and walk out?"

"All what you are saying is true but witchcraft does not work that way. Once you enter a house and touch money, you are finished."

"Is that so, what then are the benefits of witchcraft?"

"It has no benefits. Imagine, there are times when a witch aged six is asked to kill her mother. The following morning, the mother is found dead, leaving the little girl motherless."

"If that is the case then it is inhuman."

"It is inhuman indeed."

Tsotsi had an interesting story to share with Faya, his boy. "One day I boarded a minibus. It couldn't move. The driver was surprised because all along, the minibus had no mechanical fault," he started off.

"What happened when the bus failed to move?" Faya asked.

"All of us were ordered to come out. When we came out, the minibus moved."

"What happened next?"

"The driver ordered us to go in one by one. Every body got in, except me. The minibus moved. The driver took it lightly. He thought it was just a simple mechanical fault. He then allowed me in. I went in. It couldn't move. When I stepped out, it moved. I signaled the driver to leave. Inquisitively, he never switched on the engine. I, therefore, untied the white magic handkerchief. He watched fifty cows come out. They fed on the green grass along the road. Hastily, I tied them back and disappeared."

Faya was gripped with fear. He had worked for Tsotsi for well over ten years. This part of him was a secret. He was hearing it for the first time. He didn't know that his boss was a wizard. Sweat broke out on his forehead. He fished out a handkerchief from his trousers' pocket. He wiped it off.

"So, have you brought me here to help you to collect the livestock?" he asked.

"No, I have brought you here so that we may both turn into hyenas. After that, we go and steal cows. If you want to become rich then this is the best and simplest way."

"How about if you transform on your own first so that I can watch and learn from you?" he requested.

"Sure, I can do that."

Tsotsi put the brown magic stick on the ground. He jumped over it. Immediately, he turned into a hyena. He jumped over it again. He transformed into a human being.

"Have you observed how I do it?"

"Yes, boss, I have."

"Wealth is at your doorstep, Faya."

He did not appreciate the adage. He had never seen a man transform into an animal. Fear and doubt filled his heart. He thought within himself, "If I turn into a hyena, and the owner of a kraal stabs me with a spear, how will I return to this place to turn back into a human being?"

As he pondered, Tsotsi told him that they were both to jump over the brown magic stick. They had to go and return. Unwillingly, he joined his boss. They jumped over it. Immediately, they both turned into hyenas. They sped off.

Although he ran, his fears had not left him. When his fear became unbearable, he stopped and pretended to scratch his leg. Tsotsi, now transformed into a hyena, did not stop. This gave him a chance. He began to back away. When he arrived at the place where they had transformed into a hyena, he jumped over the brown magic stick and transformed into a human being.

He began to have mutinous thoughts. He asked, "What would happen if I were to run away with the brown magic stick?" He picked it up. "I am going to teach this thief a bitter lesson," he said to himself as he ran away with the brown magic stick. He disappeared.

Meanwhile, Tsotsi was successful in his mission. He tied fifty cows in his white magic handkerchief. He ran back to their meeting point. He wanted to transform back into a human being. To his surprise, the brown magic stick was not there. "Where is my brown magic stick?" he asked as his heart beat rapidly, "Maybe Faya has it, I suppose I had better wait for a little while."

Time went by. Faya did not appear. Tsotsi was at a loss as to what to do next. "This is the disadvantage of doing things with young people," he murmured to himself as he wondered what had happened to the brown magic stick. The sky got lighter.

The missing brown magic stick scared him. He untied the white magic handkerchief. He allowed the cows to return. He longed to become a human being again. But the magic brown stick was still missing. His heart beat furiously.

"If that stick isn't found, what will I do?" he murmured to himself, "If I saw the creator passing by, surely; I would ask him to stop dawn from rising." He felt sorry for himself. "Instead of increasing my wealth, I have turned into a wild animal. Woe unto me!" he cried.

The dawn kept coming. Tsotsi was now a hyena. Since hyenas don't wander around during daytime, he slunk into the forest. He feared he would be killed by hunters. When morning came, he was not seen in his village. But the fifty cows he had untied from his magic white handkerchief were spotted wandering about. The day went by and night fell but he was nowhere to be seen. Fear filled Faya's mind.

"If my boss were to find a way to transform into a human being again, he would for sure kill me. The best thing for me to do is to run away from this village," he thought within himself. He had no peace of mind. That very night, he took his belongings. He ran away.

The next morning, Tsotsi and Faya were at large. The sun rose to mid - day. The two victims had disappeared. Gani village was preoccupied with a search for them. Although they searched, the two people were not found. Nobody figured out what had happened to them.

Tsotsi's wealth began to dwindle. He had neither a wife nor a child. The only person he truly trusted was Faya who also had gone missing. There was no one to take care of his wealth. Apparently, he had no brother and no sister. His parents died mysteriously. Lightening struck their house. They were burnt to ashes.

The rumour that circulated was that he was behind their demise. He killed them with man - made lightening. Furthermore, he once had an albino wife and three children. His greed for wealth prompted him to murder them for rituals. Laziness is a killer. It prompts you to find easy ways of acquiring wealth. But the secret about wealth is not in killing albinos but hard work.

Thieves found an opportunity when Tsotsi went missing. They stole his cattle, goats and other items. Afterwards, they resorted to removing iron sheets from his house and selling them. Finally, all the wealth was gone. His house was like a ruin. Songs were composed about how he lost his wealth. Women sang of it in their dances as a lesson to those who acquired their wealth in crooked and evil manners.

Tsotsi was no longer a human being. He was now a hyena. Life was pure agony. He could not walk during daytime. He only walked during night - time. Finding food was a struggle. Sometimes, when he entered the village to steal some goats; dogs chased him. They bit him. He ran away with wounds.

The wounds made it impossible for him to go and fend for himself. Because of this, hunger took its turn. He had to wait for the wounds to heal. Healing was not something that could take a day. It took weeks. He had to go without food for weeks. It was only when the wounds had healed that he found food. He lived a miserable life.

One afternoon, when his wounds had healed, he thought of going to look for food. Hunters from Gani village were on their hunting errand. As he intensified his hunt for food, he saw the hunters. He noted that they had guns. He was terrified. He trembled with fear. He hid in a bid to scare them.

Fortunately, the hunters had not spotted him. "If I don't scare them, they will definitely kill me," he murmured to himself, "All I need to do is to jump on one of them. Bite his right hand and grab the gun." When they came close to where he hid, craftily he did as planned. The hunters were startled. They ran after their lives. He picked the gun and the bullets. He ran away.

Skilfully, Tsotsi - turned - hyena, learnt how to operate the gun. He tested it by shooting in the air. He began to lie in wait for people. He shot down women who came to the forest to gather fire wood. He hid the bodies. He waited for them to decompose. When they had decomposed, he ate them.

Gani village began to wonder at the disappearance of women who went to the forest to gather fire wood. All men agreed to go into Mkuli forest and find out the cause of the disappearances. When they approached the forest, the hyena saw them. It hid. When they neared the place where it hid, it jumped out of its hiding place and began to fire at them.

Some men lost their lives. Others escaped with bullet wounds. The issue was reported to Chief Gani. The whole village was shaken. "Do hyenas have a factory for manufacturing guns?" This was the question villagers asked. Fear gripped their minds.

Nobody was allowed to walk during night - time. The village had pit - latrines. They stood twenty meters away from the houses. Those who wanted to relieve themselves at night used plastic pails as chamber - pots. Houses had no running water system. A bore hole was located at Chief Gani's compound.

Things took a bad turn. The hyena got very wild. It entered the village during day time. It fired at people. It was a sad moment. Young, old, blind, sick and lame people were killed. Dead bodies lay scattered on the ground with blood oozing out of the bullet wounds.

Men who had guns shot back at it. To their dismay, it dogged the bullets. Instead, it chased them and bit them. When that happened, they all showed a new pair of heels. The people had ran out of ideas. The chief promised to reward handsomely whosoever killed the hyena.

The story about the ferocious hyena spread like wild fire. It reached Faya at Chibisa, a place where he had run away for his safety. "Couldn't this hyena be Tsotsi, my boss?" he asked himself. The question troubled him. He had no peace of mind. This thought kept repeating in his mind.

With a repentant heart, he took the brown magic stick. He tested it by placing it on the ground. He jumped over it. He transformed into a hyena. He jumped over it again. He transformed back into a human being. The desire to save his village grew within him. "I should go back home to rescue my village," Faya lamented within himself, "I am the reason this trouble has befallen my village!"

He left. He travelled and managed to locate the place where they transformed into hyenas. He placed the brown magic stick on the ground. He leaped over it. He transformed into a hyena. Fear gripped him. He jumped over it again. He transformed back into a human being.

"Do birds play games at birdlime?" He thought within himself. A voice whispered to him in his heart, "Gani village has no people because of you." He was surprised, "Because of me, what crime have I committed?" He heard the voice once more, "You ran away with the brown magic stick."

He noticed that time was slipping away. He jumped over the stick. He transformed into a hyena. He ran into the forest. He cried, "Huwi huwihuwi! The ferocious hyena heard the cry. It also replied with a cry, "Huwihuwihuwi!"

The two hyenas began to seek out each other. As the Faya - turned - hyena was about to cry out again, the ferocious hyena turned up. It had a gun on its paws. He was afraid. He recognised his boss, Tsotsi. But the latter did not recognise him. It never dreamt of transforming back into a human being someday.

"How are you comrade?" Faya greeted the other hyena in a hyena's language.

"I am fine thanks and how are you too?"

"I am fine."

He fell silent for a minute. He shook his tail. "Where did you get the gun from, my friend?" He asked.

"I snatched it from hunters."

"So, you know how to shoot?"

"Yes, I do. Gani village is deserted because of this gun."

Suddenly, the two hyenas started feeling very uncomfortable. They turned to the right. They saw a huge python creping towards them. It trickily pretended to sleep. It raised its head and lowered it. It did that for three times. Immediately, the two hyenas sensed danger. They quickly walked away to a safe place.

"So you mean to say that you use this gun to kill people?" Faya asked to resume their discussions.

"Yes."

"Why?"

"In the very beginning, I was a human being. But my curiosity got the better of me."

"How did it cause trouble for you?"

"I wanted to be a billionaire."

"So what happened?"

"The young man who used to work for me wronged me greatly. In fact, these people that I am killing, I am killing them so that I may kill him together with them."

"If you found an opportunity to transform back into a human being, what would you do with that young man?"

"I would kill him."

"Why not just forgive him?"

"I cannot forgive him. He has caused me great suffering."

Faya was scared. He asked, "Should there be no opportunity for you to turn back into a human being, what will you do.?"

"That is a good question. If I never ever get the opportunity to turn back into a human being, I will wipe out every human being in Gani village."

"When you are done with Gani village, what will be your next step?"

"I will go into other villages."

"You will go into other villages to continue killing people?"

"Yes, finally, I will wipe out the entire population on planet earth."

"It seems you are so bitter with life."

"Yes, I am. I told you earlier on that I was once a human being. I was so rich. I had properties. I suspect that my worker took over the wealth."

"So the suspicion that your worker took over your wealth eats you up?"

"Yes."

"Enough of that, can you demonstrate how you operate the gun?"

"Yes, I can do that."

The ferocious hyena lifted the gun. He pressed the trigger. He fired in the air. A bang sound roared in the forest. Faya was gripped with fear. He retreated. After firing in the air, he pointed the gun at Faya. "Oh! No, don't shoot me!" Faya screamed. He smiled, "Don't worry, I won't shoot you. You are my friend."

"Why do you look sad?" the ferocious hyena inquired.

"I look sad because people make me happy. If the world is beautiful, it is because of them. They are so lovely. These days, they accommodate chickens in electrified rooms. Did chickens ever dreamt of sleeping in electrified rooms?" Faya explained. The ferocious hyena burst out with a heavy laughter.

"What's funny?" Faya asked.

"The news that chickens are accommodated in electrified rooms," the ferocious hyena replied.

"What is so funny about that?"

"The funny thing is that human beings are very clever. The chickens you are talking about are not accommodated in electrified rooms out of love. The electricity and water they use are paid for. There's also a cost to the construction of the rooms. "

"But why do they accommodate them in electrified rooms?"

"They are accommodated in electrified rooms so that they can be turned into relish in future. I have been a human being before; I know how human minds work."

"Is that so?"

"Yes, by the way, do the chickens pay rent?"

"No, they don't."

"There you are, one day they will pay for it; their heads will be chopped off."

The chicken issue was over. Faya asked the ferocious hyena to follow him. He did not refuse. He followed him while they talked about other things. When they arrived at the place where the magic brown stick lay, he told his friend to stand behind the line. He took heed to the instruction. He followed suit.

"Now I want to teach you one traditional dance from my home, is all right with you?" he lied.

"Go ahead."

"Now, when I say 1, 2, 3, go! We should all jump forward."

"I will do that, my friend."

"Here we go."

"Go ahead my friend!"

"1...2...3...Go!"

Simultaneously, both of them jumped forward. Immediately, they transformed into human beings. Tsotsi stared at Faya for a moment. He trembled with rage. He roared, "Who is this one I am seeing?" He recognised Faya. His forehead wrinkled with anger.

"I am your humble servant, Faya."

"So it is you Faya? You are finished!" He threatened. His eyes popped out their sockets.

"Please, I am begging you, forgive me!" Faya pleaded for mercy.

"No, I have suffered so much because of you!" he replied furiously.

He raised his gun. Faya shook with fear. Tears welled up in his eyes. "Please, don't kill me!" he pleaded. He paid him no attention. He pointed the gun at him. "Today, you are finished. You have ruined my whole life!" Tsotsi repeated his statement with his face screwed up like he had taken malaria medication.

Tears coursed down Faya's cheeks. Droplets of sweat filled his nose. His high blood pressure increased tremendously. Just as he was about to apologise again, the gun rang out, "Bang!" Faya fell to the ground. Blood from the bullet wound flowed on the ground.

"Uuuh!" Tsotsi sighed, "I went too far. "This boy had transformed me back to a human being, why did I decide to kill him?" Suddenly, his blood pressure rose erratically. It caused rupture to brain nerves. He collapsed. Blood flowed out his nose, mouth and ears. "Birds don't play games at their birdlime," the elders had said in times past.

2

NONE OF MY BUSINESS

A wailing sound, signalling someone was in deep pain; filled the air. Rute woke up from her sleep. She listened attentively. She immediately dressed up. Suddenly, she started sweating profusely. Her husband was in deep sleep. He had knocked off late that night. She shook him. She wanted him to wake up.

A fierce domestic fight broke in their neighbour's home. Glass tumblers and cups, crashed to the ground. A man screamed, "I will kill you today!" Fear filled Rute's mind. She vigorously shook her husband for a second time. By then, he was snoring heavily like a pig.

"Wake up," Rute persistently shook him.

"Mmm!" Joni screamed.

"Come on, please wake up!" she pleaded with him.

"What is it?" Joni responded at last.

"Just wake up."

He stretched himself out. He yawned, "Aaaahhmm!" When he shook off the sleep, he heard the cry of anguish. He was not moved. "These are the usual fights, but for how long?" he murmured to himself. He scratched his head and turned to his wife.

"Why did you disturb my sleep?" he asked in a relaxed mood.

"I disturbed your sleep because we have to go and stop a fight."

"Where is the fight?"

"Our next door neighbours are fighting."

"Are these fights new to you?"

"I know that they are not new but this one is a fierce one."

Joni was thirsty. He stood up. He walked to the kitchen. He washed his hands with tap water from the sink. He opened the refrigerator. He took out a transparent bottle of water. He closed the refrigerator. He opened the bottle of water. He poured the water into a glass tumbler. Sound of water passing through his throat was heard as he drank.

After drinking, he left the tumbler in the sink. He refilled the bottle with tap water. He opened the refrigerator. He put back the bottle. He started off for the bed room. He had forgotten to close the refrigerator door. He abruptly returned. He closed it.

As he walked to and from the kitchen, the wailing sound of a woman still persisted. It was unbearable but he chose to ignore it. He returned to the bedroom. He wanted to slip back into his blankets and continue with his sleep. He was reproached by his wife.

"What is wrong with you?"

"There's nothing wrong with me, I just want to sleep."

"If our neighbour's wife was your direct sister, would you conduct yourself that way?"

"Don't ask me obvious questions. I've already told you that the fight doesn't concern me. By the way, are we experiencing this fight for the first time?"

"Isn't this the time to show that you're a human rights activist?"

"Do you want us to start a fight?"

"No, my husband, I am simply concerned by the repeated cries of anguish."

"What has my job as a human rights activist got to do with our neighbour's fight?"

"You are there to fight for rights of human beings."

"If that is the case then I won't be sleeping every night because this family fights almost daily!"

"No, my dear, you won't be doing this daily. Let us go and stop the fight!" Rute pleaded.

"Have you forgotten why they fought last week?"

"Yes, I have forgotten, can you remind me, please!"

"The bone of contention last week was tooth paste."

"What about tooth paste."

"The wife squeezed the tooth paste tube in the middle instead of the bottom when she wanted to brush her teeth."

"And that was a good reason enough for a fight to break."

"Yes, to the husband squeezing tooth paste tube in the middle is not economical," Joni replied as he burst out with laughter, "People get irritated by petty issues."

"You know what, anger is a choice. You chose to be angry or not."

Faiti's family fought almost daily. No day passed without them exchanging blows. Each time a quarrel broke, a fight followed. It would start in the bed room and continue into the sitting room. If the worse came to the worst, neighbours would watch it outside their house free of charge. After watching for a while, they would intervene and stop it.

Children in the neighbourhood enjoyed watching the fights. They gathered up and cheered. One morning when the couple had sobered up, Geja, a rude child approached them and asked, "When are you going to fight again?" The couple just shook their heads. They shamefully stared at each other. They regretted the way they conducted themselves. As if that was not enough after knocking off, Sefa, a six year old boy mocked them, "Next time you fight again, I will be your referee. I will give out MK100.00 to the winner and MK50.00 to the loser."

Faiti and his wife, Melina were a disgrace. Educated as they were, they fought like brutes that had never been to school. People have very high expectations from educated people. The conduct of a university graduate was expected to be well above that of an uneducated person. The two, were uncivilised. Fortunately, it was a new couple. They had no child.

"So what do you want me to do?" Joni asked as they resumed their discussions.

"Go and break up the fight before they kill each other."

"Do you know why they are fighting?"

"That's immaterial; our assignment is to stop the fight."

"I don't want. I am sick and tired of stopping fights of irresponsible people."

The fight continued. Sound of chairs falling off was heard. The cry of a woman in pain rang through the air. Sound of the beating was heard. It sounded as though the beating was done by use of metal objects. In the midst of the beating, a voice pleading for forgiveness was heard.

"My husband, please forgive me. Spare my life. Allow me to return to my parents alive. I am the only child in our family!" she pleaded.

Indeed it was true. She was the only child in their family. Her mother only gave birth to one child. Efforts to have other children proved futile. Herbalists as well as medical doctors tried to rescue the situation but to no avail.

"No! I can't spare your life!" a man's bitter voice replied.

"Please don't kill me, just send me back home."

"To hell with that, I will deal with you today."

None of the words that were being exchanged by their neighbours moved Joni. His wife, Rute wept. She grabbed the keys for the main entrance. She wanted to open the door and go outside to stop the fight. He grabbed her hand. He snatched the keys from her.

"Where do you think you're going?" he asked angrily.

"I want to go and stop the fight."

"Of what concern is it to you?"

"The one about to be killed is a human being like me, furthermore she is a woman."

"So?"

"I want to go save her life."

"That won't happen."

"My husband, please, allow me to go. I want to save the life of my fellow woman!"

"Do not interfere in other people's affairs."

Joni slipped into the blankets. Cries of agony from their neighbour's house continued filling the air. Rute couldn't sleep. She couldn't stand it. Her eyes welled up with tears. Watery mucus dripped from her nose. She stood on their western window. She pushed the curtain and peeped out in sorrow. She stopped sobbing. She began to weep loudly. Her husband was irritated. He woke up.

"Won't I sleep today?" he asked furiously. Rute did not answer back. She picked a yellow handkerchief. She wiped off tears from her eyes and sniffed.

"I said, won't I sleep today?" her husband thundered.

She remained silent. Her husband sucked his saliva. He covered his body with a blanket. The fight and cries of deep anguish continued. Then a groaning sound was heard. It was life's final cry. It was a cry that signalled the loss of life. A deep breath followed thereafter. The devil had finished his first assignment. The poor woman was dead.

Silence reigned as though everything was fine. But the truth of the matter was that the devil had won the fight. As the silence continued, a man's voice expressing shock was heard, "Mmm! I've murdered my wife! That's it, I will also kill myself!"

Joni slipped out of his blankets. He turned to his wife, their eyes met. Fear gripped both of them. "This is serious!" he lamented.

"My husband, can you see now what has happened!" Rute scolded as she cried.

"I was supposed to make the hay while the sun was shining!" Joni reflected on the proverb as tears coursed down his cheeks.

As they wondered as to what they should do, they heard a sound like that of a man trying to kill himself. Then they heard a thud and the final pronouncement, "I am dead!" A heavy snoring sound followed. Silence fell again. The devil had completed his second assignment. Joni was confused. He did not know what to do. Tears flowed slowly out of his Chinese eyes.

"If only I was not stubborn, I could have saved the two lives! Joni blamed himself for his stubbornness.

"My husband, we could have saved these lives!" Rute lamented as she cried. Her husband bent his head down. He buried his face in his palms. He sniffed and sobbed. He pulled his blue handkerchief from his shirt pocket. He wiped tears off his face. As he was about to put back the handkerchief, he sneezed. He wiped off watery mucus over his upper lip.

"Rute, I suggest that we move out of here immediately," Joni suggested to his wife.

"Why?"

"If we'll stick around, we will be taken as witnesses."

"Yes, you are quite right, but won't that give people the impression that we are the murderers?"

"To me the best option is to move out as soon as possible."

"If that is the case, we have to leave immediately."

In the middle of the night, Joni and Rute sneaked from their home. Since it was very late in the night they had to walk on foot. Minibuses had stopped moving. They took Ludzu road. At Ludzu Trading Centre, they booked a room at Kuza Lodge. They had to rest so that they could proceed with their trip the following day.

Morning came. The sun rose. The two semi - detached houses remained locked. Neighbours were sceptical about why the two houses remained locked. They surrounded them to try and peep through the windows. They couldn't detect anything. The matter was reported to Police.

In no time, the law enforcers arrived. They force opened Joni's house. They found nobody, but everything was in order. They force opened Faiti's house. It was horrible. Both man and wife were dead. A hammer lay beside Melina's body with her head crashed.

A mix of blood clot and brain showed up at the passage of her nose. Blood clots showed up outside her two ears. Her dress had blood stains. Her right hand had been chopped off. Her eyes were wide open as if pleading for mercy. A good part of her beautiful artificial hair seemed to have been uprooted with great force. It was horrible.

Faiti's body lay in a pool of blood. His hand held a knife that pierced through his chest into the heart. Blood covered the whole knife. His shirt and pair of trousers had serious stains of blood. His eyes were also wide open, signalling the pain he had gone through when he was taking away his life.

Portraits of the deceaseds' wedding ceremony hang on the four walls of their beautiful sitting room. Lights were on. The door leading to the corridor remained open. The wall clock was ticking on the eastern wall; probably to remind the law enforcers what time they had carried out their investigations. The puzzle was why Joni and his wife disappeared.

3

MYSTERIOUS HUMAN SKULL

Vuto was a tall, fat, strong and brown in complexion young man. He came from Deza village. He had passion for hunting. But his problem was that he was impatient. Each time he heard something, he rushed to tell it out. He had no time to scrutinise what he had heard before airing it out to people. Though he was warned several times about his character, he turned a deaf ear.

About ten kilometres from Vuto's home, stood Afuro Forest. It was a thick forest. Antelopes, hyenas, monkeys, lions, pythons, giraffes, and rhinos lived in this forest. On the eastern side, lay Chiso River. It provided drinking water for all animals of the forest. Visiting the river was scary. It was said crocodiles ruled the river.

Rumour had it that those who frequented the forest, came across cooked food. When that happened, the tradition was to eat it. After eating, plates were left on the spot. An attempt to steal them provoked the appearance of a very beautiful girl of about ten years old. "Choose between life and death!" the beautiful girl warned. But again, those who opted to reject the food, ended up failing to find their way home.

One cool day, Vuto set off for the forest on his hunting mission. While there, he came across a human skull. A cold chill ran down his spine. He wondered what might have happened for a human skull to be found lying idle. "Am I at a graveyard," he wondered. He approached it. He looked squarely at it as he rubbed his left eye. He held his mouth and yawned. He pushed it with a wooden rod.

"What caused your death?" he inquired. The human skull never replied. He pushed it for a second time, again, it didn't answer back.

"Don't you understand what I am saying?" he thundered as he pushed it with his wooden rod for a third time.

"Sir, I was killed by my mouth," the human skull replied at last.

Vuto was frightened. He retreated. He couldn't believe his ears. His hands trembled. The wooden rod dropped to the ground. His heart started beating rapidly. After a few minutes, composed himself. He gathered courage. He picked the wooden rod from the ground. He shrugged his shoulders. He approached the human skull. He pushed it.

"Can you repeat what you just said?" he requested the human

skull.

"I said I was killed by my mouth," the human skull replied. Insert chapter three text here. Insert chapter three text here. Insert chapter three text here. Insert chapter three text here.

Without wasting much of his time, he rushed back home. He explained the ordeal to Semu the chief, "Sir, I have encountered a mysterious skull."

"What is the mystery?"

"I have come across a human skull that speaks."

"Is the voice audible?"

"Yes, Sir, it is audible."

Semu was moved by the mysterious story. He mobilised his subordinates. They set off for the forest. On the way, birds entertained them with beautiful melodies. Those who were so used to the forest branched off the main path into the forest to pick wild fruits. They ran back quickly into the main path while they enjoyed the taste of the wild fruits. Monkeys jumping from one tree to another cheered them on.

At last, they reached the spot where the mysterious human skull lay. Slowly, Vuto approached it. He crossed his mouth with his first finger to signal those who accompanied him to be quiet. He pushed it with the wooden rod.

"What did you say was the cause of your death?" he inquired. The human skull never replied. He asked it for the second time but still it didn't answer back. Semu lost his temper.

"Why did you decide to fool me?" he asked with rage showing on his face.

"No, Sir. I didn't mean to fool you. I don't understand why it is not responding."

"Don't worry we'll wait for you up until it responds. Try it again."

"What if it doesn't respond?"

"Don't ask me that silly question. You brought us here to witness a mysterious human skull. All what is required is for you to prove to us that indeed this human skull is mysterious. Keep on trying."

"What, what, what death cause you?" he asked trembling. Semu and all those who accompanied him burst out with laughter.

"Vuto, your question is ambiguous. Be composed. Don't tremble. We are here for you."

"Sir, I am very sorry for fooling you!"

"So you just wanted to make fun of me?"

"No, that was not my intention."

"But what was your intention."

"My intention was for you to witness the mystery."

"Where is the mystery?"

Vuto was silent.

Semu and his contingent, returned home angry. He warned him never to fool him again. He bowed down and apologised. When they team reached home, Vuto sneaked away. He returned to the forest. He went straight to where the human skull lay. He approached it. He pushed his wooden rod.

"What did you say was the cause of your death?" he inquired. The human skull burst out laughing. It replied, "I was killed by my mouth." Vuto was perplexed. He sighed, "Incredible!"

"My simple advice to you is, watch your mouth," the skull said.

"Thank you so much for the advice. Shortly I was here with Chief Semu and his contingent, why did you refuse to speak?"

"I was shy."

"Shy, are you a female skull?"

"Yes, I am."

"Before you became a skeleton, were you married?"

"Yes, I was married."

"Married to whom?"

"I was married to Cox. He was a white man. The mistake I made was to brag about being married to him and that he was handsome."

"And what happened?"

"I was kidnapped by jealousy people and killed in this forest."

"Ooh! shame! If I brought Semu and his contingent again, will you answer me back?"

"Yes, I will."

He was excited. He whistled a tune and danced. He returned home with a lot of questions in his mind. "Is Chief Semu going to accept my invitation to come and witness the mystery again?" He stood under a guava tree to figure out how he would convince him to come and witness the mystery. He took courage and approached him.

"Sir, immediately we reached home, I returned to the forest, surprisingly, the human skull replied to all the questions that I put forward before it."

"Vuto, don't be silly! I am not your playmate."

"I am sorry, Sir. I urge you to accompany me and witness it for yourself."

"What should I do with you if the human skull won't respond?"

31

"If it won't respond, you'll be at liberty to kill me."

"Are you serious?"

"Yes, I am, Sir."

"I hope you are aware that a promise is a credit."

"I am aware, Sir."

Vuto had a sweet tongue. He was a very good narrator. Each time the village received a white visitor, he became the interpreter. No wonder he was able to convince, Chief Semu to mobilise his subordinates for a second time. They all started off for the forest. They went straight to the place where the human skull lay. With courage and determination, he pushed it with his wooden rod as he did previously.

"My dear lady, what did you say was the cause of your death?" he inquired. The human skull remained silent. He asked it for the second time. It didn't respond. "Why are you betraying me?" he asked with nervousness, "Are you still shy to answer back?" The human skull remained silent. Fear gripped him. He looked up the sky and looked down. He was shocked and confused.

"Vuto, have you ever in your life come across a human skull that speaks?" Semu asked as he started losing his patience.

"No, Sir."

"Why then do you want to cheat the world that this particular human skull can speak?"

"That is why I called this a mystery."

"Shut up! How many times have we been here?"

"We have been here twice, Sir."

"If we have been here twice, has your skull uttered a word?"

"I am sorry, Sir. It is not my skull."

"Shut up! why are you being rude to me?"

"I am sorry, Sir."

Though the weather was cool, he started sweating. The back of his white shirt and the armpits were wet with sweat. He pulled out a handkerchief from his pocket and wiped off sweat from his face. Tears flowed out of his chameleon like eyes. Watery mucus oozed out of his small nose. He sniffed in an attempt to stop the flow. His big ears stood up like those of a rabbit.

"Have you failed to chat with the human skull?" Semu asked as he looked squarely into his eyes.

"Yes, Sir."

"Do you remember the promise you made at home?"

"Yes, I do."

He made an attempt to escape. He wanted to save his life. The attempt was aborted by Bavu and Njuchi Semu's messengers. "What are you up to?" Semu inquired. "My time to live on earth has expired!" He lamented.

"How do you know?" Semu asked.

"I know because a promise is a credit."

"You are quite right. Your time has indeed expired. You can't treat me like a fool twice."

"I am sorry, Sir. Please forgive me!"

He fell down. He wept bitterly. "Stand up quickly, before we take the day light out of you!" Bavu and Njuchi warned as they held his two hands.

"Did you bring me to appreciate the way you weep?" Semu thundered with protruded eyes.

He didn't answer back. His eyes were filled with tears of regret. He tried to kneel down to plead with Semu to spare his life. "Stand up!" Bavu and Njuchi ordered. He stood up so helplessly. His chameleon eyes protruded more than normal. He sniffed continuously.

"Why did I provoke the wrath of Chief Semu?" he shouted at the top of his voice, "Sir, I beg you to forgive me!"

"Enough is enough, Kill him!" Semu issued his final verdict.

Bavu and Njuchi held him. They tied him to a tree with nylon ropes. They took turns to butcher him with a heavy axe. Just as he breathed his last minute, the human skull burst out with a mocking lady's laughter, "Hahaha!" Fear and unbelief filled the minds of Semu and his men.

"So he never lied. I have killed an innocent person," Semu regretted as he wiped tears off his eyes.

With mouths wide open in disbelief, Bavu and Njuchi stared at each other. They shook their heads as if they had horns. They watched blood gushing out of Vuto's body, the way it does out of a butchered cow. Their hearts were broken. They didn't know how to get out of this mess. A life was lost.

Bavu and Njuchi regretted having butchered an innocent person. Bavu, who had heart problems, suddenly collapsed. First aid was administered to try and save his life but to no avail. He breathed his last breath.

Njuchi's blood pressure rose. He sweated profusely. He shouted, "I am failing to breathe!" He fell down screaming, "I have killed an innocent person!" He also breathed his last. Chief Semu was shocked. The situation was tense.

"Vuto, I told you that the cause of my death was my mouth. I was warning you to watch your mouth. You have also been killed by your mouth. As for you my dear, Chief Semu, Learn to forgive. You have butchered an innocent person. The world is full of such deaths. Lives have been lost and continue to be lost, never to be recovered!" the human skull advised. It finally, burst out with a characteristic mocking laughter, "Hahaha!"

4

TAKE IT EASY

Nyadani stood before two gloomy faces, Nkhwazi the headmaster and Thobwa his deputy. He placed his two hairy hands crossed, behind his back. His teeth kept biting his lower lip. The weather was cool but contrary to that, sweat drops covered his tall nose.

Frequently, he fished out his maroon handkerchief from his navy blue school uniform trousers. He wiped sweat off his nose. His heart beat increased abruptly. Lidia his girlfriend was pregnant. She mentioned him as the man responsible for the pregnancy. But she had not disclosed it to him.

The headmaster opened his drawer. He pulled out a perfume bottle. He shook it three times. He lifted his left hand. He sprayed under his armpit. After he was done with the left armpit, he lifted his right hand. He sprayed the perfume under the armpit. Nyadani and the deputy headmaster, Thobwa watched admiringly. The aroma of the perfume filled the headmaster's office.

"Good morning, young man?" the headmaster greeted Nyadani while putting back the perfume into the drawer.

"Good morning, Sir."

"I am glad to hear that you are all right," Thobwa spoke softly as he tried to kill a mosquito that was flying over his head. Nyadani was offered a seat. He held the chair. He pulled it back and sat on it.

"Well young man," the headmaster started off, "We've decided to call you to hear your side of the story. Lidia is expectant. You have been mentioned as one responsible for the pregnancy. Can you defend yourself?" the cross - examination began.

He scratched his ball shaped head. He tacked in his shirt. He tightened the belt of his trousers. Sweat drops from his face dropped to the floor. If by chance his blood pressure was checked, it would have read so high. "Mmm!" he murmured with his eyes blinking fast. He felt so uncomfortable. Like a mental disturbed person, he stood up from his seat.

"Relax. Take it easy. Sit down," the headmaster consoled him and went ahead to switch on a desk fan. He allowed it to cool the room.

"Sir, Lidia is my girlfriend," Nyadani explained with his armpits sweating profusely.

"And that she's pregnant, do you know anything?" the headmaster inquired as he swerved his arm chair.

"No, that's news to me."

"News, as lovers haven't you been making love?"

Nyadani looked down. He didn't respond to that question.

"Answer me, haven't you been making love?"

"We ha.....ve," he replied as he stammered.

"Then why is the pregnancy issue news to you?"

"Pregnancy wasn't our intention."

"What was your intention?"

"We just wanted to enjoy ourselves."

"Pregnancy is the fruit of your enjoyment. By the way, have both of you gone for (VCT)?" he asked as he looked squarely into his eyes.

"No."

"Don't you know that AIDS is a killer?" the headmaster continued educating him about the consequences of promiscuity.

"I know, Sir."

"Are your ears placed under your feet that you are unable to hear?"

"No, Sir."

"Are you not aware that cemeteries around the country are now almost full?"

"I am aware, Sir. But to error is human."

"You are quite right, but not when that error could cost a life."

The headmaster ordered Nyadani to walk out. He turned to Thobwa and shook his head in disbelief.

"I feel sorry for that boy. He is so brilliant. He is university material,' he spoke with a broken heart.

"I feel sorry too. But I have a feeling that the girl might have reported to school with pregnancy."

"Whether she reported here with pregnancy or not, is none of our business. The truth of the matter is that they have been making love. Our task is to go by what rules and regulations stipulate. They both deserve to be dismissed," the troubled headmaster concluded.

"Isn't there anything we can do to save the situation?"

"Like what?"

"We can advise him to refuse the responsibility."

"What if Lidia was your biological daughter, would that be your advice?"

"No."

"So your proposal is based on the fact that Lidia is not your biological daughter? Don't be selfish."

"Can we shelve this discussion, Sir?"

"No, we shouldn't. We are only brainstorming."

Foot steps towards the headmaster's office were heard. Little by little the footsteps approached the headmaster's door. A knock was heard.

"Come in," the headmaster replied. The school messenger came in. He delivered mail. After the delivery, he picked the waste bucket. He walked out. A baby crying tone was heard from the headmaster's cell phone. He ignored it. It rang again for a second time. He ignored it once more.

"Let us not waste our time discussing Nyadani's issue because it is his own making. You can't serve two masters at a time," the headmaster resumed their discussions.

"You are quite right, Sir," Thobwa replied and nodded his head.

"You know what, Sir; intelligence must be guarded by good character. Nyadani is indeed very intelligent. His responsibility was to guard his intelligence. Intelligence that is not guarded is an enemy of the law."

The headmaster called for an emergency staff meeting. Members of staff assembled in the staffroom. He coughed to clear his throat. He put off his black jacket. He hanged it on a coat hanger next to his arm chair.

"Good morning, ladies and gentlemen?" he greeted the members.

"Good morning, Sir," members replied.

"Sorry for disturbing your programmes. I won't take much of your time. The issue at hand is misconduct by two of our students. Nyadani has made Lidia pregnant. Or let me be more elaborative: One morning, Lidia fell sick. She was vomiting some yellowish stuff. The school matron rushed her to the hospital. Medical examinations were conducted. Malaria test proved negative. The Medical Assistant Chidule, decided to conduct a pregnancy test. It proved positive." Members of staff sighed, "Huuu!" it was a sigh of shock. Lidia was an orphan. But to add salt onto a fresh wound, she was on a bursary.

The headmaster continued to break the shocking news, "Miss Shemeji, the school matron questioned her about the person responsible for the pregnancy. She mentioned Nyadani. Members of staff murmured. They were shocked. The culprit in question had a good character. Teachers loved him. He was so brilliant. He was always took first position in class.

"I called for a meeting to inform you that, according to the Ministry of Education's rules and regulations and in my capacity as the

37

headmaster for Gara Government Secondary School, I have dismissed Nyadani and Lidia from school forthwith."

"Excuse me, Sir," Foster, Nyadani's class teacher stood up. He objected, "I can't allow that to happen. You can't dismiss Nyadani, my super star."

"Your super - star is no longer a super star. He has ruined his future. He is now a man. He is no longer a student."

"Sir, in my own opinion you are to blame."

"Me?"

"Yes, Sir."

"Have I been mentioned as the man responsible for the pregnancy?" Nkhwazi, the headmaster asked with rage showing of his face.

"No, that's not what I mean."

"But what do you mean?"

"What I mean is, way back, health personnel visited our school to advocate for protective sex by use of contraceptives. You chased them away. If you had allowed them to conduct a health talk, we couldn't have been in this mess."

"Foster my dear, I cannot allow anyone to come to my school to advocate for promiscuity. If anything, I would advocate for abstinence. There's time for everything. Students ought to think about education and not sex."

"Can I suggest something?"

"Go ahead."

"I suggest that we dismiss the girl and not the boy."

All female teachers shouted at the top of their voices, "That's nonsense! Can a girl be pregnant without a man?"

"Yes," Foster replied calmly.

"How?" the female teachers queried.

"You know the story already."

"Which story?"

"Are you strangers to this world? I mean the story about Jesus Christ."

Once again the female teachers shouted at the top of their voices, "Ndiwe chitsiru!" ("You are a fool!")

The headmaster intervened, "Order please!" The staffroom was quiet. Order was restored. "You can go back to your classrooms. Members of staff walked out murmuring, wondering if justice had been executed. Outside the staff room, bad words were exchanged between Foster and the female teachers. Little by little, the noise faded away as they returned to their respective classrooms.

Nyadani and Lidia were invited to the headmaster's office. The two were served with dismissal letters in the presence of the deputy headmaster, Thobwa. "Since you already paid your examination fees, you'll be allowed to come and write the exams as external candidates," the headmaster concluded.

After receiving the dismissal letters, they turned and stared at each other. Their eyes met. Tears flowed uncontrollably. Watery mucus came out of their nostrils. Nyadani fished out a handkerchief out of his pocket. He blew his nose. Lidia buried her face in her palms.

"You should have known better that, it is prohibited for students to make love in school. There's time for everything. You were here to acquire knowledge and become productive citizens in future," the headmaster spoke as he showed the two heartbroken students, the way out of his office.

"Excuse me, Sir!" Nyadani intervened, "A word of thanks to both of you. What has happened here is justice at its best. Any institution is governed by rules and regulations. This institution is no exceptional. We have broken rules and regulations; therefore, justice has to take its course. I wish you all the best in all your endeavours." He waved his hand. He walked out. The headmaster, Nkhwazi and Thobwa, his deputy stared at each other in disbelief.

Outside the headmaster's office, Nyadani held Lidia by the hand. He consoled her, "We have lost an opportunity but I am sure that someday things will work out for us. They walked away from the headmaster's office. They stood under a shed of avocado tree.

"Lidia, why did you hide your pregnancy from me?"

"What would you have done if I had told you?" she replied with wrinkles on her forehead.

"I could have found a way out."

"Then find the way out now."

"It's too late."

"Do you know why I hid it from you?"

"No."

"I knew that your advice couldn't have been nothing other than abortion."

"How did you know?" Nyadani asked smilingly.

"That is what experience has revealed. When men make girls pregnant, they rush for abortion. Abortion has claimed so many lives of young girls. In some instances it has led to removal of uteruses, resulting in barrenness."

"I see, so you just decided to let both of us lose?"

"Sure."

The two students went to their respective hostels to collect their belongings. They converged at a mango tree that stood in the middle of the school compound. They waved their hands to all students who by then were attending classes.

Shock griped the other students. They all run out of their classrooms in tears. They rushed to the mango tree. They hugged them and shook their hands. They wished them well. Teachers tried to stop the commotion but to no avail. Students ran back to their classrooms after the two victims of misconduct had left.

Lidia and Nyadani headed for the bus depot which was located half a kilometer from Gara Secondary School. Apparently, they both came from neighbouring villages. Lidia came from Dziwe village while the latter came from Dambo village. Dambo bus came and since it passed through Dziwe village, the two jumped in. They left. Nyadani dropped at Dziwe bus stage. Lidia proceeded. She dropped at Dambo bus stage.

Nyadani walked to his home. He found his father relaxing outside their thatched house. Phiri his father raised his head wandering what could have brought his son home while schools were in progress. He stood up with both hands holding his waist. He buttoned his torn khaki short sleeved shirt. He scratched his baldhead.

"What brings you here?" he inquired inquisitively.

"It is a long story, allow me to drop my belongings first."

"You can do so."

He dropped his belongings in his bedroom. He came out and joined his father.

"How are you, father?"

"I am fine. Once again, what brings you here?"

"Well, I have been dismissed from school."

"Dismissed?"

"Yes, father."

His father looked up the sky like a chicken that was drinking some water. He then looked down. He sighed, "Mhuu!" He buried his head in his palms. He wept. He consoled him,   "I am sorry for breaking your heart."

"What crime have you committed?" his father asked as he wiped tears off his face.

"I have made a girl pregnant."

"Owww! an extra responsibility! you know I am as poor as a church mouse. To find school fees for you, I climb mount Malosa. I fetch firewood. I sell to the community. Your good performance gave me hope that one day you would bail out our family from poverty."

After those sentiments, he screamed and wept loudly, "Nyadani my dear son, you've let me down!" Nyadani was heartbroken. He fished out a maroon handkerchief from his pocket. He spread it on his palms. He buried his face on it. He also wept.

"Father, once again, I am sorry," he apologised.

"Nyadani, you were a God given gift to me. In you I saw someone who would in future transform our village into a town. I saw myself moving out of a thatched house into a mansion. I saw you transforming our health post into a fully - fledged hospital. I saw you transforming Dziwe primary school into a boarding primary school. I saw our village with piped water and electricity. For all this to happen, you needed to continue with your education. All my hopes are now shattered. Poverty has come to stay in our family! God, why have allowed this to happen?" Nyadani's father wept loudly once more.

"Father, I am very sorry!"

"Then what next?" he asked while turning to his son.

"I just have to leave for the city."

"You want to leave for city to do what?"

"I want go and look for employment."

"Looking for employment with a Junior Certificate?"

"Yes, what else can I do?"

"Which city are you going to look for employment?"

"Blantyre."

Nyadani lifted his head. He was shocked. He saw at a distance a girl who resembled Lidia. "Is what I am seeing true, if it is indeed true, what brings her here?" He murmured within himself. The more the distance reduced, the more the girl resembled Lidia. Finally, it was no longer resemblance but it was her in person. With a troubled mind, he stood up to welcome her. Before he could take her to where his father sat, he had to find out what brought her there.

"You are welcome," he started off.

"Thank you."

"What brings you here?"

"I have been kicked me out of my home."

Nyadani's father called him. He wanted to find out what the girl was up to.

"Who is that girl?"

"She is the girl I made pregnant."

"And what is she looking for here?"

"She came to tell me that she has been kicked out of her home."

"She has been kicked out by whom, her parents?"

"No."

"Kicked out by whom?"

"She has been kicked out by her aunt."

"Where are her parents?"

"She has no parents, she is an orphan."

"An orphan made pregnant by a boy from a very poor family, what a combination! What then have you resolved?"

"We haven't resolved anything yet."

"Know this, if she has been kicked out; I am also kicking you out of my house."

"Father, just allow us to spend a night here today. Tomorrow we will leave for job seeking in the city!" he pleaded.

"No, I am sorry, go and pack your belongings and leave forthwith."

"Father, I know I have wronged you. It wasn't my intention to break your heart. No wool is so white that a dyer cannot darken it. Allow us to spend a night here and we leave tomorrow."

"I am no longer interested in you, my son. You very well know that I am a widower. I struggle to get a day's bread. I can't even afford decent clothes and you decide to make my life more miserable! Collect your belongings and join your girlfriend."

He walked back to Lidia.

"You look so depressed, what's the matter?"

"I've also been sent out," he replied with a troubled mind.

"So what do we do?" Lidia asked as she sat on her travel bag.

"I suggest we commit suicide."

"Of all things, you choose to commit suicide?"

"Yes."

"Isn't that making the situation worse?" Lidia made a correction.

"What do you propose?"

"What if we go job hunting?"

"You propose we go job hunting with Junior Certificates?"

"We have no choice but to make do with what we have. At least we have a starting point."

"In other words, I should be looking for a job as a labourer?" he commented with a troubled heart."

"Exactly!"

"And you?"

"I'll be looking for anything, be it a nanny or a waiter. Our stupidity has granted us that status."

"Uuuu! I still insist that the best solution would be to commit suicide."

"Committing suicide is not a solution. But how are we going to do it?"

"We can drown ourselves in Chisombe River or be run on by a car."

Lidia smiled. He noted the smile.

"Why do you smile?" he inquired.

"I've just remembered an incident that happened home," she replied.

"What happened?" He inquired as he held his mouth to sneeze.

"In my village, a certain gentleman got fed up with life. He decided to commit suicide. He looked around for a rope. When he got one, he set off for Nguli forest. He identified a strong tree. He threw his rope up on a reliable branch. He tightened it. Just as he was about to tie it around his neck, a lion charged at him. "My God!" he screamed. He then ran for his life."

Nyadani burst out with laughter. With tears of laughter streaming out of his eyes, he asked, "I thought he wanted to die, why did he run away?"

"I don't know?"

"May be he was not serious about suicide."

Nyadani walked back to the veranda where his father sat. "Father, you are such a loving and caring father. You have laboured throughout your life to make sure that I have a bright future. I am very sorry for frustrating your efforts. I am now leaving to face the world head on. I wish you all the best." He stood up. He walked towards his father. He shook his hand. He waved goodbye. His father watched him walk away. A stream of tears flowed out of Muzipasi, his father.

He approached Lidia. He signaled her to stand up. She stood up. Both of them started off on foot. From Dziwe village to the city of Blantyre, the distance was 40km. It was a journey that took them one full night. By 6.30a.m, the couple was in Blantyre. They located the Labour Office. It was close to Wenela Bus Depot.

Wenela Bus Depot was a depot for buses travelling within Malawi and outside. Buses to South Africa and Zimbabwe started off from this depot. A good number of buses from this point travelled to the southern, central and northern districts of Malawi. On the eastern side of Wenela Bus Depot, was Blantyre Railways Station.

As time approached 7.00a.m, the whole ground around the Labour office was thronged with job seekers. They ranged from youth to the

43

elderly. Statistics revealed that a great number of them were youth. One elderly man stroke the attention of Nyadani. He could have been in his late eighties. He had grey hair. He wore a torn shirt, trousers and brown sun hat. He put on a completely worn out white sports shoe. It was very difficult to tell whether it was white or brown.

The elderly man had a black plastic bag. He time and again, drew out dried cassava from it. He chewed it with difficulties. He had very few teeth. He coughed frequently and spat on earth. He used his funny sports shoe to cover the saliva he spat with earth. He looked miserable. Nyadani stared at him. He was touched with compassion. He turned to Lidia. He shook his head.

"Why are you shaking your head?" Lidia asked.

"I am sympathising with that old man. Who would employ an old man like him?"

"Indians prefer to employ old men like him more than the youth."

"They employ them to do what type of work?"

"They employ them as watchmen."

"You are quite right. I have always wondered why most watchmen for Indians are very old. Why do they abuse elderly people?"

"They do not abuse them; there is a secret behind all that."

"What secret?"

"The secret is that elderly people spend most of their time dozing during the day."

"So?"

"So, when night falls they don't sleep and are able to watch for the property the whole night."

"Where did you get that revelation?"

"I got it from my father."

"In which case, if one employed a young man as a watchman he would be sleeping the whole night instead of being awake to watch for the property?"

"For sure that is what would happen."

Most job seekers at Wenela Labour Office spoke Chichewa. Here and there, other languages like Sena, Lomwe, Yao, Tonga and Tumbuka could be heard.

"Lidia, can you believe it, there is a boy here who was kicked out of the university?"

"Why was he kicked out?"

"He comes from a poor family and his guardian could not afford to pay fees for him."

"You are not serious. Is he also looking for employment?"

"Yes."

"To be employed as what?"

"To be employed in either of the following fields: Labourer, messenger, garden boy, house boy, cleaner or watchman."

"Is it true that one university student who was employed as a watch man, just to raise school fees was attacked by thieves?"

"It is true. Life is very unfair. Most intelligent students come from poor families."

"Why is that so?"

"I don't know."

"Should the creator bless me with wealth one day, I will come up with a trust to assist such students."

"That's how one thinks when poor, when riches come your way, you forget everything and greed takes over."

Two female officers approached the entrance of the Labour Office. All job seekers rushed to the entrance. "We haven't opened the offices yet. We came to clean the offices," the female officers explained.

A white Jaguar drove into the Labour Office. It stopped close to the Labour Office entrance. A young man in his thirties came out. He was wearing a blue jeans and a white golf shirt. He knocked at the door. A short female officer, dressed in purple dress came out.

"What can I do for you, Sir?"

"I am looking for a house boy and a house girl."

"What is your name, Sir?" the female officer inquired as she wrote the name in her register.

"My name is Bob."

"Bob who?"

"Bob Phoza."

"Where do you reside?"

"I reside at Namiwawa."

"And you, what is your name?"

"My name is Jean."

She invited Bob into her office. She brought out a hard cover book. She took his details. She advised him about the minimum wage for house boys and house girls. After getting the details, she invited Bob outside to where job seekers sat. When the job seekers saw Bob and Jean they all rushed to them.   Being new comers to the Labour Office, Nyadani and Lidia remained seated. They didn't know how to go about.

"Madam, are those two seated there looking for employment?" Bob inquired from the female officer while pointing at Nyadani and Lidia.

"Let me check with them."

Jean approached the couple. She greeted, "Good morning, lady and gentleman?"

"Good morning madam," they replied in unison.

"Are you looking for employment?"

"Yes, madam,"

"Follow me!"

They both stood up. They followed Jean. She entered her office together with Bob.

"Sir, these two are looking for employment. You are free to interview them," She introduced the topic for discussion.

"Thank you madam, how are you lady and gentleman?"

"Fine thank you, Sir and how are you too?"

"I am fine. To cut the story short, I am looking for a house boy and a house girl. Are you ready to go with me?"

"We are ready, Sir."

"Madam, let me not take much of your time, allow me to take these two and do the rest of the interview at home," Bob suggested to Jean.

"Welcome, Sir. Lady and gentleman, I wish you all the best."

"Thank you so much, madam."

Nyadani and Lidia came out of the Labour office. They followed Bob. He opened his car. He ushered them in. He fastened this seat belt. He advised them to fasten their seat belts as well. He switched on the engine. The car hummed. Off they went.

"By the way, I enjoy listening to stories from the village, do you have any, young man?"

"Yes, Sir."

"Can you share it with me?"

"Yes, I can. The story is about why our village has no Health Centre."

"Go ahead and explain why it is so."

"We had a Government Health Centre with well qualified personnel but all of them ran away."

"Why?"

"One night the Medical Assistant heard sounds of drum beating. He rushed to the Health Centre. He peeped through the window. He saw naked women with babies on their backs dancing. He approached the main door and opened it. To his surprise, the drum beating stopped and nobody was in the room. He trembled with fear. Immediately, he closed the door. The drum beating started again. He peeped through the window once more. The same thing happened. Naked women with babies on their backs danced. He ran away and asked for posting instructions the following morning."

"Gosh! So what happened thereafter?"

"No health personnel accepted to work at the Health Centre."

" So the structure is there but there are no health personnel?"

"So the structures are there but there are no health personnel?"

"The structures are no longer there, people vandallised them and left the health centre in ruins.

"A similar story to that one is where the Government constructed a beautiful school with a good number of beautiful staff houses. Today all the houses are vacant. All staff members moved out and opted to rent ten kilometers away from the school. But the good thing is, the houses are intact, they were not vandalized."

"Why did the teachers move out?" Lidia asked.

"They moved out because when they slept at night, in their houses, in the morning they were discovered naked outside. Sometimes the whole family would be discovered naked at the graveyard. "

"That was sad!"

"When I requested for a village story, I expected similar stories to the ones I heard before. Incidentally, what are your names?" Bob inquired.

"My name is Nyadani and she is Lidia."

"Are you related?"

"No, Sir, we just met here at the Labour Office," he lied.

Bob stopped his car outside Pep Shop. He instructed Nyadani and Lidia to come out. They came out. The car had central locking system. He locked it. He invited them into the shop. They followed him without questioning anything. He picked a trolley. It had four small black wheels. He pushed it towards female shopping area.

Bob called for a lady sales representative to assist Lidia, "Madam, can you take this girls around to do her shopping?" She smiled and replied, "You are most welcome, Sir." She took her around. She shopped five dresses, five pairs of underpants, five camisoles, four pairs of shoes, four pairs of socks, three handkerchiefs, two face towels, two bathing towels and two pairs of slippers.

"Is that gentleman your relation?" the sales representative inquired from Lidia.

"No, he is my new boss," she replied.

"Is that so, it seems he is a loving and caring person."

"That is what I have observed."

Bob took Nyadani to men's shopping area. He shopped seven pairs of trousers', seven shirts, five pairs of shoes, five pairs of socks, four handkerchiefs, two face towels, two bathing towels, four pairs of underpants and two pairs of slippers.

Nyadani and Lidia did their shopping with amazement. They wore happy faces. They couldn't believe their eyes. When they were through with the shopping, Bob picked two beautiful suitcases. The brown one was given to Lidia. The black one was given to Nyadani. After that, he approached the cashier for payment. He squared the MK 200,000.00 bill. The trio then walked out. The car was centrally opened. They went in.

"Sir, on behalf of Lidia and indeed on my own behalf, I thank you for all what you have bought for us. May the good Lord richly bless you," Nyadani extended his words of thanks before they started off.

"No mention."

Bob switched on the engine, off they went. Their next stop was outside a beautiful maroon gate. The beauty of the gate signified the beauty of the house. The gate opened on its own. The view of the house made Nyadani's heart miss a beat. It was fascinating. The house was quite big. It had a semi - detached guest wing and a servant's quarter.

The scenery was fantastic with assorted fruit trees. Slowly, they drove in. He packed the car in the double garage. He opened the car door. He came out. He opened the doors for Nyadani and Lidia. A lady, brown in complexion came out of the house. She smiled and hugged Bob.

"Welcome my dear!"

"Thank you, my angel."

"How are you our two precious gifts?"

"We are all right, madam." Nyadani and Lidia replied with wide smiles.

"Feel at home. You are most welcome."

"Thank you."

Madam relieved them of their travel bags. She ushered them into the sitting room. She proceeded into the visitors' bed room. She dropped the travel bags. The mode of dress for the two visitors clearly indicated that they came from poor families. Both of them put on worn out black school shoes. Bob sat on his favourite cream sofa that stood opposite a Plasma television screen. The screen was magnificent.

"Take your seats lady and gentleman," Bob welcomed them into the sitting room. The sitting room was sparkling. It was air - conditioned.

The ceiling was made of plaster of Paris stuff. Anything the two laid their eyes on was wonderful. Bob invited his wife for introductions.

"Meet Nyadani our new house boy. Seated next to him is our new house girl, Lidia. He then turned to the two visitors, meet my angel, Edna."

"We are so glad to know you madam," Nyadani and Lidia responded cheerfully.

Bottles of juice and packets of assorted biscuits were served. As the two were enjoying the refreshments, Bob held a remote control for the Plasma television screen. He switched it on. They watched a football match between two well - known European teams. By then Edna was in the kitchen preparing lunch.

"Sir, how many children do you have?" Nyadani broke the silence.

"I have none."

"Why?"

"We just want to make sure that we have children when we are ready for them."

Nyadani turned to Lidia, their eyes met. Both of them smiled.

"I saw you turn to Lidia and smile, do you have a story to tell?"

"Yes, Sir, we are admiring your wisdom. Most youth in my village are not employed but have children."

"These are some of the factors that have promoted poverty in our country. If you cannot feed yourself, how can you feed someone else?"

"You have to provide for yourself first before you can provide for others. I sympathise with street beggars, lame and blind who sleep under bridges in cities."

"I too sympathise with them. Our government is watching them bearing so many children and not taking a step to control them. Infact, leaving them to bear children is like seating on a time bomb."

"Is it true that these street children mobilise themselves at night and attack people at bank auto tellers."

"It is true. Edna was once attacked, since then we don't withdraw money at night."

"If they are able to do that at a tender age, what will happen when they are fully grown?"

"They will be breaking houses and banks. Let me borrow your statement: Our government is sitting on a time bomb."

"And do you know what; most call boys who flood the bus stops in cities were street children?"

"Is that so?"

49

"Yes."

"No wonder most of them are very rude."

"Exactly, a child without parental guidance is a dangerous child."

"You are quite right. I understand that they sometimes become bus conductors and drivers?"

"Yes."

"When that happens, they become naughty conductors and drivers."

"That explains it."

"Father and mother in a family act as rails on a big bridge to the children."

Lidia took the juice bottle empties to the kitchen where Edna was preparing lunch. She was directed to the dustbin where she dropped them. In the intervening period of time, Bob took Nyadani for a familiarization tour.. He wanted specifically to show him where the toilet was in case he wanted to relieve himself.

After the tour, Nyadani had the urge to relieve himself. He entered the toilet. He was fascinated by the beauty and the aroma. Everything seemed to be in place. The white hand wash basin was spick and span as if it had never been used. A hand drier was located next to it. The seat pan and the cistern all looked new. He came out. He returned to the sitting room.

Bob left the sitting room for his bed room. He came back in short trousers. Meanwhile, dinner was ready. The two visitors were invited to the dining room. They went in. All the four walls were decorated with portraits. One portrait depicted Mount Mulanje, the tallest mountain in the country. Another portrait depicted tourists enjoying their time on the shows of Lake Malawi, the biggest lake in the country.

The dining table was beautiful. It was made of glass. It had eight chairs. A hand wash basin was located on the right hand corner of the room. A mirror stood above the basin. Bob ushered the two visitors to the hand wash basin to wash their hands. He then, directed them to their respective seats.

Lidia sat on the eastern side of the room. Nyadani sat opposite her, on the western side. Bob sat on the southern side. He faced Edna. She sat on the northern side. They both seemed to be enjoying themselves. After the meal, they had a choice of fruits to eat. There was a basket with assorted fruits: oranges, apples, mangoes, bananas and peaches.

Nyadani and Lidia picked the apples and ate. Their faces were bright, an indication that they enjoyed the meal. They both picked the plates, food warmers, folks, spoons, tumblers and water jag. They took them back to the kitchen. They came back to clean the table and put back everything in order.

Nyadani and Lidia returned to the kitchen to clean the utensils which were placed in the sink. Lidia did the cleaning. Nyadani dried them with a kitchen towel. They placed the dried utensils in the kitchen unit. When they were done with the cleaning and drying, they returned to the sitting room.

Bob's house had semi - detached servants' quarters and guest wing. The servants' quarters was meant for the male house keeper and the female house keeper. The guest wing was meant for visitors. Under normal circumstance, Nyadani and Lidia were supposed to be accommodated in the servants' quarters. But instead, they were offered the guest wing. Since it was semi - detached, Nyadani chose to occupy the right wing. Lidia chose to occupy the left wing.

Bob handed over keys to both of them, "I expect you to be very responsible. Cleanliness is next to godliness. You will be accommodated in these wings, free of charge. Electricity and water bills will be my responsibility. All I can ask from you is to switch off lights and close all water taps each time you walk out of the rooms."

"Thank you so much, Sir," Nyadani and Lidia expressed their appreciation.

"No mention."

They opened and viewed one wing together. They couldn't believe their eyes. The wing had running water and electricity. It had a combined sitting and dinning room. An ivory coloured sofa set stood on the western side. A transparent dining set stood on the eastern side of the room.

The master bed room was ensuite. It had two beds. One was single and the other was double. The two beds had new mattresses and beddings. New treated mosquito nets hang above all the beds. The combined toilet and bathroom had a wall mounted shelf. A cane for refreshing the air stood on the shelf. Two white bathing towels hang on the wall mounted stainless steel towel hanger.

The wing had a kitchen. It also had a kitchen unit. A sink was located next to it. An electrical kettle and a double hot plate rested on top of the unit. A store room was located on the eastern side. It had wall mounted shelves. The shelves accommodated two units of bathing and washing soap.

Plastic bottles of body lotion stood next to the washing soap unit. 50Kgs of maize flour bag leaned against the back wall. A 50kgs bag of rice leaned against the maize flour bag. Opposite the main entrance door was a door to the visitors' toilet and the bath room. Above all, it had a geyser.

"Lidia, are we dreaming?" Nyadani asked with excitement.

"I suppose so. I can't believe my eyes, from thatched houses to a furnished guest wing!"

"What have we done to deserve all this?"

"Nothing my dear, our task is to make sure that we don't miss this opportunity."

They came out to view the other wing. They opened it. To their surprise, it had exactly the same features like those of the first wing. They walked around to view the surroundings. They were beautiful. Two guava trees stood adjacent to the two semi - detached houses. Night queen flower stood between the two wings.

"Lidia, we messed up our future but here is our second chance. What should we do?" Nyadani started off, before they departed for their respective houses.

"I propose that I abort the pregnancy."

"Why?"

"Once madam discovers that I am expectant, she would kick me out."

"If that happened, what is your problem?"

"I will miss this golden chance."

"Take it from me, abortion will take us nowhere. If madam discovers the pregnancy and kicks you out, I will be there for you. Who knows, you might be carrying the future president of our country."

"Promise me that you will not let me down."

"I am responsible for your pregnancy. Come rain, come thunder I will be there for you. For things to work for us, we should avoid committing murder."

"You are quite right."

"The baby you are carrying has not committed any crime. It doesn't deserve a death sentence. It has the right to live."

Nyadani strategised how they would keep their secret, "It would be right and proper for us to maintain the secrecy. You shouldn't put on tight dresses. We have to work very hard and be good time keepers. Winning the hearts of our masters is the key to our success. We have to be royal and obedient. Once they build trust in us, everything will be all right with us."

"I totally agree with you. If only we can win the hearts of our masters, we are guaranteed a bright future."

Nyadani left Lidia's wing. He went to his wing. He slept. Morning came. They woke up very early. They took their bath. They reported for duties in good time. Madam welcomed them. She prepared breakfast for them. They were   introduced to their day to day assignments. By the time Bob woke up, the house had been cleaned. He was impressed. He called Nyadani.

"I am impressed with your work, keep it up!"

"Thank you, Sir."

"By the way, you speak good English, what is your secret?"

"My English teacher had a very good command of English language."

"And you imitated him?"

"Yes."

"That explains it. But what happened for you to go job hunting?"

"My father failed to pay school fees for the last term."

"Did you register for the examinations?"

"Yes, I did."

"And how far did Lidia go with her education because she also has a good command of English."

"I don't know because we just met at Labour Office and we didn't go into those details," he cheated.

"Find out from her this evening."

"I will do that, Sir."

Bob and his wife Edna left for work. Nyadani and Lidia were left to look after the whole house. The day watchman came to greet Nyadani.

"How are you?"

"I am fine thank you and how are you too?"

"I am fine."

"Sir, what is your name?" Nyadani inquired.

"My name is Chipolopolo," he replied.

"I am happy to know you, Sir."

"And you, what is your name?" he asked.

"My name is Nyadani."

"Do you smoke?"

"No."

"Why?"

"Smoking is hazardous."

"I see. What about beer, do you drink?"

"I don't either."

"You are a very strange young man. Most of your age mates smoke and take spirits."

"Let them take the spirits, what they forget is, they are damaging their lever and brain. Give it another ten years from now, mental cases and deaths will be rampant. Lever failures will be a common disease throughout the country. Youths who have gone full throttle into consuming that deadly stuff look older than their age. They stagger even when they are sober. Their lips look reddish like a sliced watermelon. "

"You are absolutely right."

"The following are the effects of alcohol consumption: - Abdomen and legs swell causing severe pain. Veins in the lower esophagus and spleen enlarge. Stone like particles develop in the bladder and the end result becomes lever cancer."

"You seem to know a lot."

"Yes, I do."

"You have educated me about the lever, what about the brain?"

"The effects of alcohol to the brain are: Memory impairment. Blurred vision. Slurred speech. Difficult in walking and slow reaction time."

"You are not serious!"

"I am serious. Those who consume alcohol are infact making an application for the mentioned diseases."

"You are quite right."

"But you know what, developed countries have age limit for one to start consuming alcohol."

"That's true."

"What about our dear country, Malawi?"

"I don't know. Apparently, what I have observed is that the majority of those who take that deadly stuff are youths."

"It's a shame!"

In the evening, Bob and Edna knocked off from work. On their way, they discussed the fate of Nyadani and Lidia. They were very much concerned about their ages. What struck their minds most was the fact that they were form four students who couldn't continue with their studies due to poverty.

"My dear, our new house boy registered for form four examinations but failed to continue with his education because of poverty, how can we assist him?" Nyadani asked his wife.

"What about the house girl?"

"I don't know how far she went with her education,"

"Her situation is similar to that of the house boy."

"How then can we assist them?"

"We can look for places for them at Njelu Private Boarding School."

"That is a brilliant idea. They are too young to finish as a house boy and a house girl."

"I totally agree with you."

"Let us find out from them, if they are willing to go back to school."

By and by, they reached their house's gate. The gate swung open. The watchman saluted. Bob in turn, saluted back smilingly. The watchman put on a very nice uniform. It comprised a white shirt, black trousers, leather boots and a khaki cap. They drove in. He parked the car in the garage.

Nyadani and Lidia welcomed them. Nyadani took Bob's briefcase while Lidia took Edna's hand bag. They left the briefcase and hand bag in the sitting room. They came out to collect the items they had brought. Amongst them, were bread, assorted fruits and cooked fresh maize. The items were taken to their respective locations.

The house was cleaned. It looked sparkly. Bob patted Nyadani on the back, and congratulated him, "Well done. The house looks nice." He replied, "Thank you very much for your compliments." Bob winded up the discussion, "The pleasure is mine."

Lidia was busy in the dinning room preparing tea. When everything was ready, she invited them in. They all one by one, walked towards the hand wash basin. They washed their hands. They dried their hands with a blue towel. It was hanged on a towel hunger next to the basin. They sat at the dinning table. They took the tea with some snacks.

When they were through, Nyadani and Lidia cleaned the dinning table and set it, in readiness for supper. Edna prepared the meal. She was exhausted and wanted an early sleep. Food was brought in. Nyadani and Lidia excused themselves. They wanted to take the meal after their boss and mistress had finished eating. "Join us," Bob extended an invitation to them.

Edna came in. She walked towards the hand wash basin. She opened the tap. She washed her hands. Her husband followed suit. Nyadani and Lidia washed their hands last. As they ate, Bob looked squarely into Nyadani's eyes.

"My brother, my wife and I have a proposal to make. Both of you are free to take it or leave it," Bob started off his address.

"You are welcome, Sir."

"Both of you are young. You registered for your school leaving exams. We have agreed to send you back to school. We'll send you to a boarding school. The two wings you are occupying will remain your homes. Do you accept this offer?"

"We do, Sir."

"If you accept, we offer you this place as your permanent home. We will be doing everything for you."

"Thank you so much, Sir."

After supper Nyadani and Lidia returned to their wing. They couldn't understand what was happening. To them this was a dream come true. They agreed to take a shower first and afterwards converge in Lidia's wing to strategies. They left for their respective wings. In no time, both of them were ready for the discussions.

"Lidia, we've been given a second chance, how do we handle it?" Nyadani opened the discussions.

"We have to handle it with care. Our own relations rejected us. The coming in of this family to assist us is something we shouldn't take for granted."

"That is true, but how many months is your pregnancy?"

"Three months."

"Can you attend classes for a term without problems?"

"Yes, I can."

Footsteps were heard outside the wing. They stopped their discussions. They wanted to attend to whoever came to meet them. Nyadani opened the door. He walked out. He saw the watch man doing his usual night inspections. He walked back into the wing. He closed the door. He felt thirsty. He went into the kitchen. He came back with a glass of water.

"Who was it?" Lidia asked.

"Futi the watch man, he is conducting his usual night inspections. I like his name. It is so short. The day watch man's name is quite long."

"What is it?"

"His name is Chipolopolo."

"And the night watchman's name is Futi?"

"Yes, in English language, the meaning of 'Futi' is gun while the meaning of 'Chipolopolo' is bullet."

"So Bob and Edna, our boss and mistress respectively, have a gun and a bullet? Lidia commented with laughter.

"Yes, I am just wondering, was it a coincidence that the watchmen have such funny names?"

"I have no doubt that it was just a coincidence."

"Well, back to our discussions, where did we stop?"

"We stopped at whether I would manage to attend classes for a full term."

"That's right; you said you can attend classes for a full term. If that is the case then, let us take the offer seriously."

"You are quite right. We shouldn't miss this golden chance."

"Let me go to sleep. In the morning we will hear from Bob what arrangements they have made for us. Good night!"

"I also wish you a good night."

Nyadani opened the door. He came out. He closed it. He walked towards his wing. He fished out a key from his shirt pocket. He opened the door. He went in. Straight he went into his bedroom. He slept. In the morning both of them woke up very early. They cleaned their boss's house. Lidia prepared the breakfast. As usual, Edna woke up early than Bob.

"Good morning, lady and gentleman?" she greeted.

"Good morning madam," they replied in unison.

"How was the night?" she inquired.

"In was wonderful," both of them replied."

"What made it wonderful?"

"The generosity you have accorded to us," Nyadani replied.

Don't worry, we are there for you. You are the future leaders. It is our responsibility to equip you with knowledge so that you would contribute positively to our country's development."

"If that mentality was in every Malawian, our country could have developed tremendously. Our problem is greed. There are people who have billions of Kwachas in their bank accounts but watch a fellow Malawian drop out of school due to poverty or die of hunger," Nyadani commented.

"The spirit that makes me mad is the spirit of stealing. People believe that without stealing you can not prosper in life," Edna spoke with a soft voice.

"You are quite right. It is a pity that people think that way. The truth of the matter is that one has to sweat to find something. Work has to come first for one to be successful. It is only in the dictionary that success comes before work. It is so because of alphabetical order," Nyadani winded up their discussion.

Bob came out of the bedroom. He put on a nice black suit, a white shirt and well - polished black executive shoes. He had a black bow tie on his neck. He looked smart. He greeted Nyadani and Lidia. He then proceeded to the dining room. He took his breakfast. He checked his wrist watch. The time was 7.00a.m. He stood up from his seat. He returned to the bedroom. He collected his brown briefcase. He came out.

"Edna sorry for the inconvenience, you should use the small car because I want to rush to Njelu Private Boarding School to find places for our dear ones," Bob spoke as he headed towards the main entrance door. He waved at Nyadani and Lidia. They waved back. Edna rushed to open the door.

"That's all right, dear. I wish you a nice day."

"I wish you too, a nice day," he replied. They hugged and kissed each other."

Nyadani and Lidia grew up in the village. They never saw their parents hug and kiss each other in public. It was doubtful if at all they even did it in secret. Probably it could be because they never brushed their teeth. They couldn't afford toothpaste. When they saw their boss and mistress kiss each other, they shied away. They laughed.

"Why do you shy away and laugh?"

"In my home village, it is a taboo for people to hug and kiss each other in public," Nyadani explained.

"We grew up with the same mentality. But with time we learnt that there's nothing wrong in hugging and kissing your loved one. Why should you kiss each other in secret, is it a crime?" Edna cleared the misconception.

"Our culture is very secretive. That is why AIDS spreads like wild fire. Father and son cannot discuss sexual issues. Sons learn sexual matters from fellow youth who in most cases are ill mannered. A man goes into marriage without knowing what marriage is all about. At least women take their time to discuss marriage issues with girls. Knowledge about marriage is one sided, hence conflicts in most marriages."

"Nyadani, where did you learn all that?" Edna quizzed him. He smiled shyly and replied, "I read it in the Newspaper on a marriage column."

"I see, I was wondering how someone of your age would know all that."

"I like reading Newspapers."

"That's good, what about you, Lidia, what is your hobby?"

"I like reading as well."

"That is great! As students you ought to fall in love with books."

"Madam, how far did you go with your education," Lidia opened up and inquired.

"Why ask me that question?"

"I've asked that question because I see you as role model."

"Well, I have a doctorate degree."

"Wow! That's wonderful. What about our new dad, Bob?"

"He also has a doctorate degree."

"I am encouraged. I will also work very hard so that I obtain a doctorate degree."

"You will be granted the desires of your heart by the creator. Let me take leave. I hate reporting late for duties."

"But before you go, which university did you graduate from?"

"We are both graduates from Mantoba University in Canada."

She waved at them. They waved back. She headed for the main entrance. She opened the door. She came out. She closed it. A raving sound was heard. She hooted and left. Nyadani and Lidia stared at each other for a moment. They were challenged by their bosses' achievements. "If they made it, what would stop us from making it?" Lidia thought aloud.

Bob and Edna were fluent English language speakers. Nyadani and Lidia enjoyed listening to them speak. They imitated them when they were not around. Nyadani became Bob and Lidia took the role of Edna.

"Good evening my angel?" Nyadani greeted Lidia.

"Good evening my dear."

"How was your day?"

"It was marvelous and you?"

"It was splendid."

After the imitation, they held their palms. They walked around the sitting room. They hugged and kissed each the way Bob and Edna did. Thereafter, they all burst out with a heavy laughter. "That is how it will be in future when both of us become graduates," Nyadani commented with enthusiasm.

When Bob and Edna held their discussions in another room, their accent was exactly that of the whites. It was lovely. Their parents were diplomats in US. They were family friends. During festivals they spent their time together. Exchange visits were common between them. That is how the two came to know each other.

As youth, the couple was not so close to each other. Bob was a friend to Bruce, Edna's brother. Actually, they had a sister and brother relationship. How things twisted, nobody understood. Their meeting in the university just cemented their parents' relationship, as family friends. They both came from wonderful families, no wonder they also had a wonderful family. A healthy fruit tree bears good fruits.

Bob had an assignment. He had to visit Njelu Private Boarding School.

It was one of the best schools in the country. All universities that existed were flooded with students from that school. He drove to the school where he found classes in session. He parked his car outside the headmistress's office. A guard with a long beard, advised him to park at visitors' car park and not at the headmistress's car park. Interestingly, the headmistress had no car.

He reversed the car. He parked it as advised. He came out. He walked to the headmistress's office. He knocked at the door. There was no response. He knocked again for a second time, but still there was no response. As he was about to knock for the third time, he heard a female voice behind him, "Go in, Sir."

Bob turned backwards. He saw a young lady in her late twenties. She had deep - black artificial hair. It looked so natural. She was smartly dressed. She put on an ivory - cream suit with a blue scarf. The aroma of her perfume filled the whole office.

"Take a seat, Sir," she welcomed him.

"Thank you, Madam."

The headmistress pulled her chair towards the table. She sat down. The school radio was on. She reached it with her left hand. She was left - handed. She switched it off. She sneezed. Later, she coughed. She excused herself. She wiped her nose with a purple handkerchief. She brought out a writing pad ready to take minutes of their discussions.

"What can I do for you, Sir?" she inquired.

"I have two students to be admitted in form four," he replied after clearing his throat.

"Form four?" the headmistress asked surprisingly.

"Yes, form four."

"We have one term to go so we can't entertain new comers."

"These ones you are going to entertain," Bob replied courageously.

"What is so special with them?" she inquired as she looked squarely into his eyes.

Bob narrated the whole story to the headmistress. She was moved with compassion. She, therefore, enrolled them. She handed over the brochure to him. He browsed through it. He checked the cost for the whole term. He nodded his head, an indication that the cost per term was manageable to him. She noted the nodding of the head. He pulled out a cheque book from his briefcase.

"I understand that enrolment fee for one term is MK 200,000.00 per student, isn't it?" Bob inquired.

"Yes, Sir."

"Is boarding fee inclusive?"

"Yes, it is, Sir."

"What about school uniform?"

"It is inclusive as well."

He placed the cheque book on the table. He flipped the cover to access one leaf. He pulled out his executive pen from his shirt pocket. On the right hand side of the leaf he wrote the date for that day. He wrote the amount of school fees in words followed by the amount in figures.

Bob signed at the bottom of the leaf. "Not negotiable" were words written at the top of the leaf. He signed along the words. In so doing, he opened the cheque. He handed it over to the headmistress. She placed her first finger at the door of her right ear. She shook it to stop the irritation. She stared admiringly at Bob. She smiled.

"If only we had one million people like you in our society, this world could have been a better place to live. But alas! It is filled with greedy and self - centred people. People who enjoy exploitation," she expressed her appreciation.

"That's true, madam. Let us hope for a total overhaul of our values."

"Let us hope so."

"When can I bring the two students to start learning?'

"Bring them tomorrow."

"Thank you so much for your positive consideration. Let me take leave. I should be bringing the students tomorrow."

"By the way, how did you identify the two students?"

"I identified them at Labour Office. They were looking for employment. My wife and I realized that they were young and we decided to send them back to school."

"You are a very nice person."

"I appreciate your sentiments."

"I hope I will not be infringing on your rights!'

"You can go ahead."

"I don't know where to start from."

"Start from the beginning."

"Are you married?"

"Yes, I am happily married to my sweetheart, Edna and you?"

"I am still single."

"Take it easy, your future husband is on the way."

"Can I take your phone number?"

"What for?" he asked suspiciously.

"I need your phone number for communication purposes."

"I get the point. Here you are: - +2650888336853."

Bob stood up. He pushed his chair backwards. He extended his hand to her. She stretched out hers. They shook hands. She stood up. She walked towards the door. She opened it. He came out. She smilingly watched him come out with an admiring eye. He closed the door. He walked down the steps that led to the visitors' car park. He opened his car. He went in. He switched on the engine. He took off.

Throughout his journey, he whistled his favourite tune. On his way back, he noticed that the number of mental disturbed persons in the streets had increased. Most of them were youth, in their teens. Why it had increased, was a subject of discussion with Edna; his wife. Bruce, Edna's brother; was a Psychiatric Doctor.

Nyadani and Lidia were admitted to Njeru Private Boarding Secondary School. He picked them for shopping. He parked his car at Chichiri Shopping Mall. They went into Game Shop. It was congested since it was a Wednesday. It was a tradition that Wednesdays prices for commodities were slashed down.

Bob signaled Nyadani to collect a four wheel trolley. They walked round and round, picking groceries and stationery for school. Nyadani and Lidia kept staring at each other in dismay. After picking all what they required, he paid off the bills at the Till. Nyadani pushed the trolley out of the shop to where the car stopped. They loaded the goods in the boot. He took the trolley back to the shop. He returned. They took off for home.

"We just don't know how to thank you Sir," Nyadani started off as they travelled.

"Don't worry; I am doing exactly what my parents did for me. I don't have children yet. I need to be practicing parenthood. Who knows, you might be the only children we have to look after on this planet earth."

"Up until now, we are failing to comprehend what is happening. It seems as if we are dreaming. It is as if, we are no longer on earth and that we are on another planet. We were kicked out of school and our hopes were shattered. Our relations rejected us. We looked at ourselves as materials fit for burial at a cemetery. You came in and rescued us."

"You have a goal to accomplish before you leave this world. We are there to assist you to achieve that goal."

"You came in when we needed help most. You are our God given angels."

In the evening, all arrangements for Nyadani and Lidia's departure for school were made. They had supper together. Bob revealed his future plans for the two students. He promised to take care of them from secondary school to university. The two wings they occupied would remain their permanent homes. He again promised to visit them every month end. He would bring them groceries and find out about their progress from the headmistress.

"I have secured places for you two at Njelu Private Boarding School. I will drop you tomorrow. My plea is, please work very hard. My wife and I, are willing to see you through your secondary and university," Bob broke the good news.

"Lidia and Nyadani, I will miss all. Both of you have wonderful characters. We are optimistic that you won't let us down. I wish you all the best," Edna spoke as she wiped of tears of joy from her eyes.

"Most of the times I dominate to comment, this time let me give chance to Lidia," Nyadani excused himself.

"Thank you for giving me a chance to talk, mine are words of appreciation for what you have done and you continue doing for us. Our relations failed to see us through our secondary education due to poverty. You've given us hope. We promise to do the best and be selected for university studies," she spoke with her small voice. She wiped off tears of joy that flowed through her right and left dimples.

Nyadani and Lidia left for their wings. They slept. In the morning they winded up all preparations for their trip to school. Bob delegated Edna to go and drop them. They parked their belongings inside the boot. They got into the car and took off for Njelu Private Boarding school. It was an hour's drive. She parked the car at the visitors' car park. They all came out. They headed for the headmistress's office. Edna knocked at the door.

"Come in!" a female voice replied. They all walked in. Edna was offered a seat while Nyadani and Lidia remained standing with their hands crossed behind their backs. The headmistress switched off the radio.

"How are you Madam?" she greeted.

"I am fine and you?"

"I am also fine."

The headmistress turned to Nyadani and Lidia. She greeted them and came back to Edna.

"Madam, what can I do for you?"

"My husband came here yesterday to secure admission for two students who are standing beside me."

"Who is your husband, Bob?"

"Yes, Madam."

"The two students are welcomed, you can return."

"Thank you. But before I leave, these two students already registered for their examinations at Gara Government Secondary School, how will you handle their issue?"

"We will inform the National Examination Board and make arrangements for them to write here."

"I appreciated Madam, thank you so much."

Edna stood up. She bid farewell to the headmistress. She waved her hand at Nyadani and Lidia then walked out. The two students were now offered seats. They were served with a pamphlet of rules and regulations. They read through and handed it back. She hummed a tune. She called the National Examinations Board Executive about the two students. Arrangements were made. They were cleared to write the examinations at Njelu Private Boarding Secondary School.

"You are welcome to Njelu Private Boarding School. You've read the rules and regulations for yourselves. I am told that your sponsors are not your relations. I urge not disappoint them," she cautioned them.

She gave them school uniforms: A white shirt and a blue trousers for male students and white blouse and a blue skirt for female students. She called for the school messenger, Gazi. She instructed him to look for the School Matron and Patron. They came in. She instructed them to escort the new students to their respective hostels to drop their luggage.

Nyadani and Lidia came out of the headmistress's office. It was then that they remembered they had forgotten some of their luggage in the mistress's car. As they were contemplating of what to do, they saw her driving in. She parked at the school car park. She dropped the luggage. She left. The patron escorted Nyadani while the Matron escorted Lidia to the hostel. They both dropped their luggage. They put on school uniforms.

Njelu Private Boarding School had two streams for form four students, 4A and 4B. Nyadani and Lidia were directed into form 4B. The class had 40 students. The coming in of two new students increased the number to 42. The class room was situated on the western side of the school compound.

The classroom had an orchard behind it. Around it, grew assorted types of flowers that made the outside, look beautiful. Flowers around the school compound were watered by students who misbehaved.

Student's toilets stood twenty metres away from form 4B. They were also cleaned by ruthless students.

The class - teacher's name for form 4B was, Joga. He was slim and tall. He was light - brown in complexion. His lips were red and thick. He had a big rectangular head with small ears. He had a swollen face and legs. He laughed frequently even when there was nothing funny. The belief was that he behaved that way because he was a genius.

He always put on a long grey jacket. It looked like a dust coat. Its arms were very long. His fingers were buried in it. He wore a worn out and very short pair of blue jeans trousers. Students nicknamed it, "I can't come down. I am afraid of dust." Around his waist, ran an old worn out black leather belt. Its wear and tear resembled a human being's skin rash.

Nyadani latter learnt that the funny - looking character was the famous mathematics teacher. Students enjoyed his subject and did very well in their final examinations. Most of them got selected for university studies.

Joga was so far the best mathematics teacher the school has ever had. Two of his former students were lecturers in Mathematics at Khola University. Other secondary schools invited him for part - time teaching. He was indeed a genius.

The other side of him was that, he was addicted to alcohol. He couldn't teach without taking the stuff. Whenever he was sober, he trembled like a patient with fever. His trembling stopped immediately he took a sip. He had readily available spirit sachets in all his jacket pockets.

He usually sneaked each time his alcohol levels had dropped. No wonder, when one came close to him he smelt alcohol. He staggered even when he was not drunk. Intermittently, he murmured to himself. More often, he spoke at the top of his voice. Saliva splashed out of his mouth each time he spoke, especially when he tried to stress a point.

Njelu Private Boarding School form four class, had weekly tests. Nyadani and Lidia reported for classes in the middle of the week. The tests for that particular week were administered. To everybody's surprise, the two new students did very well. Nyadani took first position while Lidia took second position. The class - teacher congratulated them and urged them to keep it up.

From that week on, Nyadani maintained his number one position in the weekly tests. When month end came, Bob and Edna visited them. They were so excited with their performance. They brought groceries and stationery. Other students watched them chat with their sponsors in the visitors' room.

After the chat, Bob and Edna were taken around the school campus. They wanted them to appreciate the beauty. With his phone, Bob took photographs of the scenery. He took photographs of Edna, Nyadani and Lidia.

Bob handed over the phone to Edna to take photographs of Nyadani, Lidia and him. They visited both hostels. They were clean. The headmistress spotted them walk around the campus. She came to greet them.

"Why couldn't you pay a courtesy call?" the headmistress asked as they shook hands.

"We didn't want to disturb you. You are quite a busy person. Besides, it is a weekend you need rest," Bob replied politely.

"You came to visit the two wonderful students?" she inquired.

"Yes, Madam. We are impressed with their performance. We look forward to their university selection."

"I have no doubt; they will make it for university studies. They are brilliant students."

"All I can ask from you is to keep a close eye on them. You should be monitoring their behaviour," Edna chipped in.

"I will do that. Enjoy yourselves. I wish you a nice journey back home. I have to attend to other issues."

"Thank you very much Madam for enrolling these two students in your school. You were so cooperative the day I came and here we are now with two university materials."

"No mention, you had a role to play and I also had a role to play. I have learnt a lot from you. I will emulate your good example. We do come across intelligent students who drop out of school because of financial constraints. We watch them go and do nothing. Be assured that I have joined your band wagon." After those sentiments she waved her hand and left.

It was now getting dark. Bob and Edna had to leave. They hugged Nyadani and Lidia. They walked to their car. Before entering the car, Edna opened the zip for her hand bag. She brought out two envelopes. She handed them over to Nyadani. She then joined her husband in the car. The car raved. They sped off. Nyadani and Lidia opened the envelopes.

"Wow! what is in your envelope, Lidia?"

"A very beautiful card and MK 50,000.00 pocket money, and you?"

"The same thing, I feel that Bob and Edna are not human beings but angels."

"You are quite right. What have we done to deserve all this?"

"We haven't done anything."

They read the messages on the two cards: "We love you and we will continue to love you. We are proud of you. You are our special gifts." Nyadani stared at Lidia for a while without uttering a word. Lidia too, stared back. They were lost of words to thank their boss and mistress. Both of them walked back to their respective hostels.

"Nyadani, you have very wonderful parents," Loti, his roommate spoke admiringly.

"You can't believe it, those are not my biological parents,"

"You are joking!"

"I am not joking. I am saying the truth."

"How come they love you so much?"

"That is what I fail to understand."

Examination time closed in. Teachers were groomed to revision. They brought in past papers. They wanted students to practice on. Two weeks to the exams, teachers stopped teaching. More time was allocated to studies.

Some students grouped up and indulged in discussions while others studied in the school orchard. Forms 1 and 3 students were sent on a quick holiday to avoid disruptions. Final examinations were administered.

"Nyadani, how were the exams?" Lidia inquired.

"They were fair and you?"

"They were fair as well."

"Any hope for university selection?"

"Yes, I have no doubt that I will make it for the university."

"If that is the case, I will also make it."

The school organised a farewell party for the form fours. The school hall was decorated with natural and artificial flowers. Instead of serving supper at 7.00p.m, it was served at 6.00 p.m. The party was scheduled to start at 8.00 p.m. till dawn.

At 8.00 p.m., students gathered in the school hall. All members of staff with their spouses except the mathematician, sat at the high table. This was an opportunity for the students to know their teachers spouses. They were inquisitive to see the wife of Joga, the mathematician. He never came.

The disco equipment stood at the far right hand corner of the stage.

One loud speaker stood on the right hand side while the other stood on the left hand side. Both loud speakers faced the students. The headmistress stood up. She addressed both the teachers and the students. She then declared the dance open. She came down from the stage with her short spouse. The disc joker dished out a song. They took the floor.

Mrs. Brenda Lamba, the headmistress hugged her husband. They danced to the cheering of the students. Members of staff and the students, joined in with hand clapping. Other teachers with their spouses also took to the floor. The cheering and hand clapping by the students increased.

Suddenly, heavy shouts of joy filled the air. There was commotion. The mathematician appeared on the stage. He was dressed in a khaki overall. He was wearing a black neck tie. Students shouted at the top of their voices,"Joga!" He placed his palm on the right knee. He danced round and round as if he was lame. The cheering increased spontaneously. In no time, he vanished into thin air. The packed out school hall sighed, "Aaaah!"

Calm and order were restored. Teachers and students took the floor. They enjoyed themselves till dawn. In the morning as students were ready for take off, an assembly was called. They all converged in the school hall. All teachers wore sombre faces. They were astonished. Dressed in black dress and regalia, the headmistress made her address.

"We have sad news for you," she started off, "Our dear Joga is dead. He died in his sleep." All students sighed with grief, "What a great loss to the school! The whole school wept.

A police van came. It collected Joga's remains for postmortem at Dambe Government Hospital. The revelation was that he died due to excessive intake of alcohol. The remains were brought back. Teachers and students gathered at his house to pay their last respect. One by one teachers and students entered his house. They viewed his remains.

The mathematician lay still cold in his coffin as though he was just in a deep sleep. Students and teachers wept. The best mathematics teacher the school has ever had was gone.

Joga was the only educated person in their family. He had three sisters and four brothers, all were illiterate. Alcohol took away the family's pillar. After viewing, the body was ferried to Ndiche village his home where burial took place the following day.

Nyadani and Lidia returned to their hostels. They packed their luggage ready for take off. They bid farewell to fellow students who had no transport money. They left for their homes on foot. Some travelled long distances of about ten kilometres while others five kilometres. Bob drove straight to Nyadani's hostel. He picked him. He proceeded to Lidia's hostel. He picked her and off they went.

"How is Madam?" Nyadani inquired as they sped off.

Bob smiled. He replied, "She's fine and looking forward to seeing you all. By the way, what happened to the mathematician?"

"He died in his sleep." Nyadani replied.

"Was he sick?"

"No, he wasn't sick; in fact he attended the farewell party last night."

"That's a big loss to the school. What was the revelation from postmortem, if at all it was conducted?"

"The revelation was that he died from excessive alcohol consumption."

"Was he an alcoholic?"

"Yes, he was. He nicknamed himself as D.D.N.M."

"What does it mean?"

"It means: Daily Drinker Never Miss."

Bob burst out laughing. He commented, "Intelligence without good character is lost intelligence."

"Can you repeat what you just said, Sir?"

"I said that Intelligence without good character is lost intelligence. Good character is the key to success. When I was in primary school, we had a brilliant pupil. He always took first position in class."

"What happened to him?"

"He was a bully and got dismissed from school."

"Is he still alive?"

"Yes, he is. The last time I saw him was when I was passing by the Zobwa City Cemetery."

"Where was he working then?"

"Actually, he called me from the cemetery and when I asked him what he was doing there, he proudly said that he was the caretaker."

"Gosh! life is so unfair, someone who used to take first position in class ending up as a cemetery caretaker."

"Make sure that you guard your intelligence with good character. Surprisingly, the cemetery caretaker was so proud of his job."

"He was proud of being a cemetery caretaker?"

"Yes, he boasted that he had many people under him.'"

"Which people, the dead?"

"Yes."

Bob, Nyadani and Lidia burst out with laughter

"You know what, misfortune at times makes you behave abnormally, anyway, Lidia, how were the exams?" Bob winded up the discussion about Idirisa.

"They were fair."

"Will you make it for university studies?"

"I hope so."

"And you, Nyadani?"

"The exams were fair and I look forward to university selection."

"That is great! I trust you will all make it for university studies. Going by your performance, I have no doubt you'll make it."

"I am optimistic that I will make it for university studies." Nyadani spoke emphatically.

Time flew, university selection was out. Both Nyadani and Lidia got selected to study Bachelor of Education at Chancellor College. It was in the course of waiting to leave for their studies that Lidia's pregnancy became an issue. She wanted to go on with her education but she was due for delivery.

"Nyadani, what can we do with my pregnancy?"

"We have no choice but to reveal it to Bob."

"What if he decides to kick me out?"

"I am sure he won't. I will be open with him and reveal to him exactly the situation we are in."

One cold evening, Nyadani booked an appointment with Bob. The two sat at the sitting room. Windows were closed. The air - conditioner was switched on to warm the room. The television set was switched off.

"Yes, my dear brother, how was the day?" Bob greeted Nyadani.

"It was nice and you, Sir?"

"It was nice as well. What can I do for you?"

Nyadani narrated their story to Bob. He listened inquisitively. He kept nodding his head.

"And how is the situation as of now?"

"She is due for delivery."

"To cut the story short, don't be scared. We all make mistakes. The creator created us with strength and weaknesses. We are there for you. All I can ask from you is for us to strike a deal."

"What deal, Sir?"

"Allow us to adopt the baby. We will employ a nanny to take care of it while both of you continue with your studies. For your information medical examinations conducted on Edna revealed that she can never bear children."

"Is that so?"

"Once you accept the adoption, nothing will change. Both of you will continue to live with us. We will not allow you to live together. If anything you will be allowed to get married when you'll be done with your university studies and that you are employed."

"Thank you so much, Sir."

Nyadani explained to Lidia what they had discussed. Lidia was excited. She couldn't believe her ears. All her fears were gone. They both accepted the adoption as one way of showing appreciation to their master and mistress for coming to their rescue. Edna also accepted Bob's suggestion to adopt the baby once it was born.

Lidia gave birth to a baby boy. Bob and Edna named him 'Mphatso'. The baby was adopted according to the agreement. A nanny was employed to look after the baby. Nyadani and Lidia left for university studies at Chancellor College popularly known a, Chanco. During holidays, they returned home; where the two wings were reserved for them.

On completion of their four years studies, they both graduated with Bachelor of Education Degrees. Nyadani passed with distinction. He was offered a scholarship to study Masters Degree at Huddersfield University in the United Kingdom.

Nyadani's performance was beyond compare. It earned him another scholarship to do a Doctorate Degree in Education. He successfully finished his studies. He returned home as Dr. Nyadani Muzipasi.

Nyadani and Lidia tied the note. Lidia worked for Save the Men, a Non - Governmental organization, as the Director while Nyadani worked as the Principal for Phenipho University. Bob and Nyadani now became family friends. They visited Lake Malawi during weekends and had fun together.

One weekend, Nyadani and his wife visited his home village, Dziwe. He had never been there since he was kicked out by his late father. While there, nobody recognised him. He introduced himself to people who surrounded his air - conditioned car.

"You are welcome, our son," the Chief Dziwe welcomed him.

"Thank you, Sir."

"You resemble your late father so much. What do you do for a living?"

"I am the Principal for Phenipho University."

"How come, I thought you dropped out of school?"'

"You are quite right. I dropped out of school. A certain family sent me back to school. I finished my secondary education. I got selected for university studies where I got a scholarship to study abroad. As I am talking to you now, I am Dr. Nyadani Muzipasi," he broke the news.

"Wow! My village is lucky. We had been looking for educated people like you to represent us in Parliament," Chief Dziwe expressed his happiness.

"Unfortunately, I am not interested in politics," Nyadani replied as he wiped off sweat from his face.

"It has nothing to do with your interest in politics. The term politics might be scary to you, all I am saying is that we are looking for someone who would develop our village, that's all."

Nyadani turned to Lidia who sat next to him. Their eyes met. She smiled. Nyadani's late father's sentiments when the pregnancy issue reached his ears were, "I was looking forward to seeing you completing your school and come back to develop our village." He requested to visit the cemetery to view his late father's tomb.   Accompanied by Chief Dziwe, they left for the graveyard.

It had a thick forest. It had natural trees and fruits. The boundaries had mango trees. Red, blue and white birds flew from one tree to another. They sang beautiful songs. Species had a hiding place. The exchange of oxygen and carbon dioxide between them and the trees was wonderful.

Nyadani admired the preservation of the forest. Nobody dared to cut the trees. Dried leaves and branches from the trees made the soil very fertile. Heat had no access to the soil. There were no traces of soil erosion. Greenhouse gases were absorbed, whereby reducing global warming. Rainfall was absorbed and water vapour was released into the atmosphere.

"How I wish all mountains had thick forests like this!" Nyadani commented.

"How I wish too. Drought could have been eliminated," Chief Dziwe agreed with Nyadani.

"What I fail to understand is why people fail to plant a tree when they cut one!" Nyadani continued expressing his feelings.

"In actual fact, not plant one tree but to plant ten trees after cutting one."

"You are quite right. The end result would have been a forest ten times the one that we are seeing now."

"That's it!"

"But what is the problem?"

"The problem is lack of patriotism. We don't love our country. Cutting one tree and planting ten more is not an issue. Our minds are engulfed with a destructive spirit that is why we indulge in wanton cutting of trees."

"Since people fear tampering with cemeteries the solution is to turn all mountains into cemeteries."

"That's a crazy idea but I think it would help solve deforestation problems. Can I suggest something?"

"Go ahead."

"The best solution to solve deforestation problem as far as I am concerned is for you to become our MP."

"What does the term MP stand for?"

"t stands for Member of Parliament."

Nyadani burst out with laughter.

"Is there anything funny?"

"Yes, Sir."

"What is it?"

"I have never dreamt of becoming a politician in my life. Actually politics is a dirty game."

"Infact politics is a dirty game when those who play it, are dirty."

"But as I have rightly said, I have never dreamt of joining politics."

"That is what life is all about. I never dreamt I would be Chief Dziwe, but here I am."

"Well enough of that, now back to our agenda of tomb location."

Nyadani and Chief Dziwe walked from one tomb to another. They couldn't locate his father's tomb. Tears flowed out of his eyes. He fished out his handkerchief. He wiped off tears. The chief noted it. He never commented anything.

"Sir, what about my mother's tomb, can it be located?" Nyadani inquired as he continued wiping off tears from his eyes.

"It can be located."

"Can we locate it?"

"Yes, we can."

Chief Dziwe retreated. He held Nyadani by the hand. He directed him to the tomb. His mobile phone had a camera. He took it out of its casing. He took three snapshots from different angles of the tomb. He put back the phone. The chief joked, "Were you trying to call your late mother?" Nyadani smiled, "No Sir, I was just taking pictures of the tomb." Chief Dziwe replied, "Don't worry, I was only joking."

"Okay, what about my late grandfather and grandmother's tombs, can they be located?"

"Yes, they can be located."

"How is that so?"

"It is so because, when your late father was alive, he took care of those tombs. Every year after rains, he visited the graveyard and cleared the bush. That left the tombs locatable. He picked stones and put them around. He bought paint and wrote down names for easy identification. In your case, since you left this village as a student, you never returned to trace your father's tomb."

"The problem is, my father died while I was in US."

"What do you mean by US?"

"I mean United States of America?"

"Is that so?"

"Yes, Sir."

"So the shortcut for United States of America is US?"

"Yes, Sir."

"You mean to say that you studied in America?"

"Yes, indeed. I was in America for seven years."

"Is your wife a black American?"

"No, she is a Malawian from our neighbouring village, Dambo."

Chief Dziwe took Nyadani around the graveyard. He bowed his head down. He felt sorry for himself. Indeed the two tombs for his grandfather and grandmother were located. "So it's only my father's tomb that can not be located," he thought within himself. He wept.

Back from the graveyard, children surrounded Nyadani's vehicle admiringly. As he passed by, they begged, "Sir, next time you come, buy us a foot ball." He nodded his head. He waved at them. He proceeded to visit what used to be their house. It was all in ruins. Cassava plants, pawpaw and mango tree grew inside the ruins. He buried his face in his palms. He wept.

"You know what my son, when you are young, you don't value your home up until when you are fully grown," Chief Dziwe told Nyadani.

"I get the point, Sir."

Nyadani and Chief Dziwe walked back to the vehicle. One unruly child Chopi, shouted, "Sir, give us some money!' the chief shouted at him, "Shut up! Don't be a nuisance! Sorry Sir, that is why we want you here as our Member of Parliament. We want you to arrest ignorance and poverty."

Nyadani and Chief Dziwe shook hands. They hugged each other. He opened the door of his car. He sat on the driver's seat. His wife came out. She also shook hands with the chief. She handed over an envelope labeled MK 500,000 to him and bid farewell.

Lidia returned to the car. She opened the door. She went in. She closed it. Nyadani also closed the driver's door. He raved the engine. Slowly, the vehicle started off as they waved their hands. The whole village escorted the car chanting, "Hounorable Nyadani! Hounorable Nyadani! Our Member of Parliament is leaving!"

Time for Member of Parliament elections came. Nyadani was approached to contest.

"I hope you remember what we discussed the first time we met?" Chief Dziwe inquired as they took soft drinks at Khadwa Lodge.

"No, I don't."

"If you don't remember, I will remind you."

"You are welcome to do so."

"The first day you visited the village, I expressed my wish to have you as our Member of Parliament."

"Now I can remember, Mhu! go ahead."

"Today I called you just inform you that the whole village is interested in you becoming their Member of Parliament."

"Is that so?"

"Yes, our hounorable," Chief Dziwe replied with a wide smile.

"I am not there yet, but what was my response that time?"

"You said you are not interested in politics."

"So what else do you want to hear from me?"

"I am pleading with you reconsider your response."

"Well, give me time."

"The whole village is waiting for the positive response today."

Though Nyadani tried to resist, Chief Dziwe convinced him to join politics. Under the influence of the chief, Dziwe village voted for him. He won the elections. He, therefore, resigned as Principal for Phenipho University to serve his constituency.

Nyadani was a hard worker. He enjoyed his job. It didn't take long; the president noted his excellent performance. He was given a ministerial post. He was the Minister of Education. His background as an academician, gave him an edge.

Chisomo, his secretary, prepared a familirisation tour programme to different secondary schools. She handed it over to him for editing. He went through it as he enjoyed his coffee. Incidentally, the first secondary school to be visited was, Gara. He called his secretary.

"What prompted you to come up with Gara Secondary School as the first school to be visited?" he inquired.

"Nothing Sir, is there anything wrong with that arrangement?"

"No, there is nothing wrong; only that it is the school that I attended. I misbehaved and got dismissed."

"Is that so?"

"Yes."

"Should I change the programme?"

"No, leave it as it is."

The day for the tour came. As minister, he was chauffeur driven. His driver was dressed in a black suit. He put on a black cap. He took off from Hill Capital to Gara Secondary School for his first assignment. He was warmly welcome.

The School Headmaster, Nkhwazi and his Deputy, Thobwa, took him around the school. He visited hostels for boys and girls. He also visited the Library and the kitchen. Thereafter, he was entertained to traditional dances.

Take off time came. Nyadani's Chauffeur opened the car door for him to enter. He ordered him to close it. He walked back to the headmaster's office. He was ushered in. He was offered a seat. He sat down.

"Sir, we welcome you once more," the headmaster welcomed him.

"Thank you so much, Sir. Mmm! where is Foster?"

"Foster our fellow member of staff?"

"Yes, Sir."

"He got a scholarship to USA, way back. He never returned. He is now a USA citizen. He married a white lady. He has three children, two boys and one girl. Is he your relation?"

"No, but he was my class - teacher."

"Your class - teacher, where was that?" Nkhwazi inquired.

"Here at Gara Secondary School. I knew that you never recognised me. I am Nyadani Muzipasi, a student you dismissed way back after making a girl pregnant by the name of Lidia."

Eyes of both the headmaster and his deputy opened. They recognised him. Their hearts were filled with fear and shock. They raised their hands up. They knelt down. He stood up. He walked towards them. He pleaded with them to stand up and take their seats. They took their seats. Both of them fished out handkerchiefs from their pockets. They wiped off tears from their eyes.

"Cool down, please! I am your pride. You kicked me out of school because I misbehaved. You had to go by the rules and regulations that governed the institution. Let by gones be by gones," he cooled them down.

"Sir, we are very sorry for what we did," the headmaster apologised.

"I repeat, cool down! I leave you with three cheques: MK 5,000,000.00 for infrastructure development, MK 300,000.00 to be shared between you two and MK 200,000.00 to be shared amongst the rest of the members of staff."

He handed over the three cheques to the headmaster. With a wide smile, he hugged the headmaster. He went ahead to hug the deputy. Tears of disbelief flowed slowly out of his eyes. He fished out his handkerchief. He wiped off the tears.

He walked out of the headmaster's office under the escort of the two gentlemen, the headmaster and his deputy. They were dressed in black suits with white shirts and blue neck ties. They approached his ministerial vehicle, a black Benz. He shook hands with them. Once again, he hugged both of them. Tears from his eyes run down his cheeks. His chauffeur opened the door for him to go in.

The chauffeur saluted the minister. He went in. The door was closed. Slowly, the vehicle started off. He slid the glass. He waved both hands. A river of tears flowed out of his eyes. With mouths wide open, the headmaster and his deputy, waved back. The vehicle disappeared.

5

TIME IS LIFE

Mathafu's predecessor, Mahafu, maximised all his company privileges. He was picked and dropped home daily. His kids were also picked and dropped at school. During weekends, he took his family to the lake using company's car and driver.

As if not enough, his wife was at liberty to call for the company car to take her to have her hair plaited during working hours. The driver had no time to rest. He was always on the road. Sometimes he would be sent to the grinding meal to have the maize ground.

"Love, I fear for your life," Ellen, Shoti's wife started off as they took breakfast.

"What about it?" he inquired.

"You do not rest; you are likely to suffer from hypertension."

"You are quite right, but I have no choice. Apart from being my boss's driver, I am also his wife's driver. She calls for the car to take her to the saloon to plait her hair."

"What?"

"You heard me!"

"Is your boss aware of that?"

"Yes, he is. Infact, it is him who issues instructions."

"Isn't that abuse of resources?"

"It is but that's how wasteful people are."

As time went by, Mahafu received posting instructions to Zobwa. He tried to resist but the head office stood its ground. Upon his posting, Mathafu replaced him as the General Manager for Barzing Electrical Services. He inherited his predecessor's privileges.

Unlike his predecessor, Mathafu chose to use his personal small silver vehicle to and from home. He used the company car for office duties only. Sometimes he would opt to use his personal car for office assignments. This did not go very well with the Junior Managers.

Backbiting took its turn. "Our new boss is holier than God," the junior managers made rude remarks about him. They feared he would remove their privileges. Contrary to their thoughts, he allowed them to use company cars as stipulated by the regulations. He was so meek. He had a sense of humour.

"Sir, why do you disgrace yourself?" Beata, Mathafu's secretary inquired as she brought coffee one morning.

"How do I disgrace myself?"

"You disgrace yourself by driving a small car as opposed to those posh cars driven by your juniors."

"I see! is that what you call disgrace?"

"Yes, Sir."

"I do not disgrace myself, what you have to know is, life is not a competition. Life is just an experience one has to go through."

"Sir, you are the top most boss and you deserve a more posh car than your juniors. As a matter of fact, that is your entitlement."

"I get your point, but can you imagine how much we could have been saving if all the managers had small cars and stopped using those posh expensive cars. Do you realise that there are millions of people out there who sleep on empty stomachs."

"You are quite right, Sir."

"Incidentally, a car is just a quick means of travelling, although to most people it signifies wealth."

"That statement, Sir is an eye opener to me."

"A reservoir tank with too may leakages cannot store water. Even if it had only one hole, with time, the small leakage would empty the whole tank. For our company to survive, we need to seal all holes through which we lose money. If your monthly income is MK500, 000 per month and you spend MK 1, 000,000.00, you are bound to go bankrupt, infact, someone who earns MK 50, 000.00 per month and spends only MK 25, 000.00 is better off than the latter."

"I agree with you, Sir. My neighbour had a better job than me. He earned three times my salary but he was always in debt. Every month he came to me looking for assistance. He was no better than a beggar yet he had a better salary than me. He had two posh cars but his family would go without food. That is what happens when one's priorities are upside down."

"Don't waste your time trying to impress other people. Waste your time to impress yourself. Beggars my dear, remain beggars. The beggars you see in the streets have been there since I was in primary school. Ever wondered why Africa is still poor yet it has all the resources to enable it to be a wealthy continent, the problem is, it has turned itself into a professional beggar. Do you know that the beggars we see in the streets make a lot of money every day? Some of them make as much as MK 10, 000.00 per day. If you multiply that by 30 days it means they make MK 300, 000.00 per month yet still remain poor. Interestingly, most people who assist them have very low salaries yet they excel in life. The secret of life is in giving, not receiving."

"That reminds me what my cousin said the other day."

"What did she say?"

"She said if we were to exchange countries with the Japanese and they left everything intact in their country and come to occupy our country, by the end of one year Malawi would be so developed than Japan to the extent that we would be asking for assistance from it."

Mathafu burst out with laughter. "That's right! Bad attitude is our problem. A bad attitude is like a flat tyre, unless you mend it, you can't go anywhere. We are short sighted. We have no vision. We are lazy. We love handouts."

The coming in of the new boss made Shoti the driver, to relax. He took advantage of his coolness. He developed a tendency of reporting late for duties. On several occasions, the head driver cautioned him but he never changed. He was daft.

"Shoti, if I were you, I would make sure that I don't misbehave. You had been complaining about the character of your old boss yet now you don't seem to appreciate that you have a nice boss. These days you have time for your family. Why do you report late for duties?" the head driver reasoned with him.

"I am sorry, Sir," he apologised.

The official reporting time for duties was 7.00a.m. Shoti always reported late for duties yet he was the General Manager's driver. He comfortably reported for duties at 8.00a.m. When the worse came to the worst, he reported for duties at 9.00a.m. His character, prompted his boss to sometimes drive alone. Friday, the human resources officer, invited him to his office. He verbally warned him about late coming. He promised to change but never lived by his words.

One morning, he was late for work as usual. With his two hands in his pair of trousers pockets, he walked to the carport where the General Manager's car was parked. He went round it to check if all the tyres were intact. He also checked for a spare tyre. All the tyres and the spare tyre were intact.

He fished out a work suit from his travel bag. He removed his neck tie and long sleeved shirt. He removed his black shoes and put on the work suit. He put back the black shoes. He opened the door for his boss's car with his remote control key. He went in. He pulled the bonnet lock. He came out and opened the bonnet. He unscrewed the radiator cover to check for water level.

After checking the water level, he unscrewed back the radiator cover. He pulled out the oil level stick. He cleaned the oil level stick with a waster to take the readings. He put back the oil level stick. He cleaned dust and oil stains with a waster on the engine, He closed the bonnet. He then cleaned the external part of the vehicle.

He opened the drive's door. He took a seat and closed the door. He switched on the ignition switch. Attentively, he listened to the sound of the vehicle. He switched on the wipers and cleaned the windscreen. He switched off the wipers and the ignition switch. He came out and locked it. Tholo, the messenger approached him.

"Good morning Shoti," he greeted.

"Good morning, Tholo. What can I do for you?"

"The General Manager would like to see you."

"Okay, I will be there in a moment."

Shoti put off his work suit. He put on his blue shirt and a blue neck tie. He visited the bathroom to check on the mirror if the neck tie was done correctly. He came out. He rushed to the General Manager's office. The secretary greeted him and ushered him to the General Manager's office. He knocked at the door.

"Come in!" the General Manager replied.

He walked in with hands crossed behind his back.

"Take a seat on the sofa set," the General Manager welcomed him.

"Thank you, Sir."

The General Manager swung his executive chair to the right. He stood up. He stretched both hands up and yawned. He walked slowly towards the sofa set. He stretched his hand to greet Shoti.

"How are you?"

"I am fine, thanks and how are you, Sir?"

"I am also fine."

Mathafu, the General Manager took his seat. He loosed his brown neck tie. He turned to Shoti and spoke with his deep voice, "I called you just to thank you for your hard work. I love the way you dress yourself. You always look smart. You are a gentleman." Shoti smiled and replied softly, "Thank you, Sir."

Mathafu opened his file. He took out a paper and handed it over to Shoti. "I want you to read point number five on that paper," He received the paper and read point number five quietly. "I want you to read it loudly," Mathafu advised him. "Point number five reads: Reporting for duties late is misconduct liable to dismissal," he read out loudly.

"You have heard for yourself. You are a hard worker but a late comer. You always report for duties very late and knock off very early. If we were to be deducting the hours you miss at work from your salary would you describe that as fairness or hard heartedness?"

"Sir, I am very sorry, I am going to try my best to change. I will be reporting for duties in time."

"That would be all right. But can I ask you something?"

"Go ahead, Sir."

"If a company manufactured 3,000 bottles per hour at a cost of MK100.00 per bottle, how much money would it be losing if the operator for the machine came late for two hours and knocked off two hours early?"

"Sir, provide me with a pen and a paper for the calculations," Shoti requested. Mathafu provided him with a pen and paper.

"What was your favourite subject in school," Mathafu asked realising that he was taking too long to do the calculations.

"English, Sir."

"Don't bother to do the calculations. All I wanted was for you to appreciate that time is money."

"Thank you, Sir."

"Time is life, so make sure that you keep it."

One sunny and clear morning, Shoti was late for work. The General Manager arrived for work in good time. Suddenly, he fell to the ground. He collapsed. The only person with authority to drive his company vehicle was his personal driver. Keys for the vehicle were locked in his office. He was nowhere to be seen.

People began to inquire as to his whereabouts. He could not be traced. He had deliberately switched off his mobile phone. He had a tendency of switching off his mobile phone each time he knew he was late for duties. Time ticked by. The General Manager was still unconscious. There was no other car available to transport the manager to the hospital. The head driver, who could have rescued the situation, was out to his village to visit his sick mother.

Unperturbed, Shoti appeared. When he heard that the General Manager had fainted, he sprang into action. He ran to his vehicle. Some members of staff carried the patient to the vehicle. They laid him on the rear seat and off they rushed to Kings Referral Hospital. Others shook their heads and wondered why their colleague reported late for duties everyday.

"Why did you delay in bringing this person here?" Dr. Mwayi asked when they arrived at the hospital.

"Sorry doctor, I reported late for work!" Shoti revealed.

Dr. Mwayi took his stethoscope. He placed it in his ears and with the other end; he moved it over the General Manager's chest. He shook his head. He looked up to the heavens. He sighed, "Hmm! When important people like him die, it breaks my heart!"

The doctor tried the best he could to save the life of Mathafu but to no avail. A life was lost. The cause was nothing other than, poor time management. Shoti felt sorry for himself. "How I wish I had reported for work in time! Poor time keeping is a killer!" his heart echoed with another thought. Tears flowed out his eyes.

"Companies are closing down because of people like you!" Dr. Mwayi spoke, "You have killed a man because you weren't on time. We have drivers with your attitude here at the hospital. They report late for duties and knock of early. If we were to get statistics of how many patients have died due to a similar mistake, you would be shocked! Instead of rushing to pick up a maternity patient by ambulance, they run their own errands, until the life we were supposed to save is lost."

"I won't ever be late for work again!"

"Yes, true although that may be; but a life has already been lost. It cannot be returned to us. Westerners have a saying, 'Time is money,' but me, a black man say, 'Time is life.'"

"So does this mean that my General Manager is dead?"

"Yes, this is it, he is dead" Dr. Mwayi explained, "You know what; your company can not do without a General Manager. Arrangements, therefore, have to be made immediately to call back the transferred General Manager."

"Gosh!" Shoti sighed, "So Mahafu will be called back to Kabula!"

6

SHE TOOK THINGS FOR GRANTED

Grey stood at Blantyre Bus Stands with Mwira, his wife. They were coming from Chira Hospital. Their little girl, Mwete had malaria. She slept under treated mosquito nets. How she contracted malaria was a mystery. Her body temperature was very high. She complained about a severe headache. She sweated heavily.

"Mwira, is it not last month that Mwete was again diagnosed with malaria?" Grey spoke with a broken heart.

"Yes, indeed."

"Where did we go wrong?"

"Probably the mosquito nets were treated with fake drugs."

"You sleep with her under the same net yet you've now gone into a fifth year without contracting malaria."

"That is what surprises me."

Grey had a habit of poking his nose with his first finger. No minute past without doing so. His wife hated it. She made sure that she monitors that behaviour. As they stood at the bus stands she noted that her husband was on it again. She held his hand and pulled it away from his nose. He smiled with shame.

Interestingly, Mwira had also a habit of biting her finger nails. After checking her husband on nose poking, she started biting her finger nails. Her husband noted it. He held her hand and pulled it. She burst out with laughter.

"I pity our daughter," Grey spoke as he swerved his head left and right.

"You pity her on what?"

"Your habit is biting finger nails and mine is nose poking, she might end up inheriting both habits."

"God forbid! I can't imagine these two bad habits being in one person.'

"I can't imagine it as well, poking the nose and after that, biting finger nails."

"It would be like taking out trash from the nose into the mouth."

"It would be a health hazard."

"God forbid!"

"But do you know what, that's how every human being discovered that mucus tastes salty."

"Yes, you are quite right. All of us have tested mucus at one time or the other."

"Do you know the best treatment for eye irritation?"

"No, I don't."

"It is saliva."

"Where did you learn that from?"

"One day I had an eye irritation. I didn't know what to do so, I applied saliva."

"How did you do it?"

"I cleaned it with running water and applied saliva."

"And the irritation stopped?"

"Yes, it did."

"Has it been proven scientifically?"

"No, but that's my revelation. Scientists are free to prove it. Since then each time my eye irritates, I apply saliva and it works."

As they chatted, a lady in a blue skirt came by. She had applied silver lip stick on her lips and red cutex on her finger nails. She had nice looking artificial hair. She swiftly walked towards Grey. She shook his hand and proceeded to Mwira. She came close to her. With a wide smile, she held her hand.

"How are you, my dear? she greeted.

"I am all right and you?"

"I am fine."

The lady looked squarely into Mwira's eyes. She asked, "You seem not to recognize me."

"You are quite right."

"You should be joking."

"No, I am not joking."

"Where did you go for your secondary education?" the lady inquired with shock.

"At Mifumu Government Secondary School."

"And you cannot recognize me?"

"Don't forget it is some twenty years ago. Just remind me who you are."

"Well, I am Rita."

"Rita Mbewe?" she screamed.

Since they left school twenty years ago, the two had never met. Rita was very slim as a student. Now she had put on weight and had grey hair.

"What are you doing for a living?" Mwira asked

"I am a housewife and you?"

"I am also a housewife." "You know what; there are more house wives than house husbands."

"You are quite right. How many of us ladies would stand having a house husband?"

"We wouldn't stand that; such a husband would be the talk of the town."

"That's true. Men are not as talkative as women."

"But why is that so?"

"Because we were created to woe men and that is why we are called woe - man (woman)?"

"You are not serious!"

"I am joking. The other reason could be that we are both female and male."

"What do you mean?"

"Our friends are only males but we are also males with a fee."

"Can you repeat what you have just said?"

"Our friends don't have a fee. We are called fee - males (females)."

"Probably that is why we are so expensive to maintain?"

"I suppose so."

"I am joking."

After the chat, Rita left. Mwira looked at Grey. She remembered the grave mistake she had made. She didn't introduce her husband to her friend. "Sorry, I forgot to introduce you to Rita, my schoolmate," she apologized. "Don't worry, it happens." It could have been a different story if she was a man," Grey replied calmly.

For reasons best known to mini bus owners, Nkolokosa buses weren't efficient. For well over one hour, they waited in vain. The Soche bus came. Mwira suggested that they take it. Her husband disapproved of that. Grey yawned. He stretched up his hands.

"How I wish we had our own vehicle," he murmured.

"What type of a vehicle, a wooden one?" Mwira commented jokingly.

"Do wooden vehicles exist?"

"I don't know."

"Then why mention it?"

"I just thought that's the one you are waiting to buy."

"Is that so?"

"Yes, I do admire ladies who are married to rich men with mansions and posh cars," Mwira expressed her feelings boldly.

"I also do admire men who are married to rich women with mansions and posh cars," Grey reversed the statement.

While the conversation was on, a newspaper seller came. He was advertising that day's paper. Grey fished out a wallet from his pocket. He took out MK 450.00 from it. He bought the paper. The paper's headline read: Cashgate scandal. A picture of two gentlemen in handcuffs covered a quarter of the front page. The two gentlemen in handcuffs seemed to have tried to dodge the camera man. They looked so depressed.

"Huh!" Grey sighed.

"What's the matter?" Mwira inquired.

"This guy on the right hand side of the page was my college mate. He was so brilliant," Grey pointed at the handcuffed gentleman on the right hand side of the page.

"For him to be handcuffed, what happened?"

"I haven't read the story yet. But one thing for sure is that he is a millionaire."

"I just heard from my neighbour that government monies have been plundered."

"Not by a graduate like him."

"Infact, it is the educated people who have been involved in that scandal.

"If the educated people resort to stealing, what will the uneducated do? I pity our country. The whole essence of sending children to school is to remove ignorance. Resorting to become an armed robber after walking through the corridors of a university is a serious disease that requires psychiatric treatment."

"I agree with you. That is indeed a mental problem."

Grey looked at his wrist - watch, it was 11:00 am. Normally that was the time Mwete their daughter took her lunch. This meant that anytime she would start giving them problems. As he was contemplating of going into one of the shops to buy her a thing to bite, from nowhere, a tall, slim girl, brown in complexion approached them.

"So I am at last lucky to meet you!" she thundered. She greeted Mwira and came to Grey. She gave him a shake. To his dismay, she didn't release his hand. She now held him by the arm. A shake does not go that far. This was something more than it.

"I had been looking for you," she started off.

87

"You had been looking for me on what grounds?" he asked amazingly.

"Yes, for you. You are the father to this kid on my back," she answered back courageously.

"Are you sure you know me?" he asked.

"Yes, I know you," she replied.

"Am I not a mistaken identity?"

"You are not a mistaken identity."

Grey almost burst out with laughter but he had to restrain himself. She looked serious. Mwira moved away. She was shocked and disappointed. He looked at her, she also looked at him. Their eyes met.

"Calm down my dear, I for sure, do not know this girl. It's possible she is mentally disturbed, or I am a mistaken identity," he backed himself.

"You know her. There's no smoke without fire, besides are you the only man around here, why has she chosen you?" she responded with hate showing on her face.

The girl held Grey's hand firmly. She couldn't release it. "I am Mole, I won't let you go," she threatened. He felt very bad. She was determined to make him miss his bus.

The Nkolokosa bus came. "Hey you, leave me alone. I want to go home!" he shouted. She couldn't release his hand. She held him firmly. Mwira with a broken heart, jumped into the bus. The bus left. Indeed Grey missed the bus.

People surrounded them just to watch the free wrestling. They were quite an entertainment to those who waited for buses at the stage. Rude remarks were aired out by the call boys, "Don't release him, why did he sleep with you?" He had to hold his temper and find out a solution to the hot soup he was dragged in. He continuously wiped sweat off his face.

"By the way, what do you want exactly from me?" he asked her.

"I want money to support your child and me," she replied.

"But I don't know you."

"Then how come I have your child?"

Angrily, he pushed his hand into his pocket. He fished out MK2, 000.00. He threw it at her. She quickly bent down. She picked it. She stared at it and smiled. She released his hand. Immediately, she vanished into thin air. People stared at him as if he had four eyes.

The Soche bus came. Grey boarded it. Fear of another

embarrassment, he no longer waited for the Nkolokosa bus which usually dropped him close to his house. He dropped at Manda stage. He walked to upper Chitawira where his house was located.

He knocked at the door. Mwira saw him. She did not come to open it an indication that he was not welcome into the house. He knocked for a second time. She didn't open it. She instead ordered Mwete to go and open it. He got in. He discovered it was tense in the house. Mwira's face looked like the face of a boxer.

"Good afternoon, love?" he greeted her. She didn't answer back.

"What's wrong?" he inquired. She stood up from her seat. He retreated.

"I didn't know that you are a wolf in sheep's skin," she thundered with rage showing on her face.

"Mwira, hold your tongue. I swear before God that I do not know that girl," Grey backed himself. She looked at him and clapped her hands. "If you never knew all this time who I am, you'll know me now," she threatened.

She opened the sideboard. She broke all the tumblers and cups. She collected all her husband's suits from the bedroom. She burned them. Grey watched not knowing what to do next. Tears flowed out of his eyes. He loved Mwira, his wife so much. After breaking the tumblers and cups, she took a hammer and smashed the television set. She walked towards her husband.

"Do you want me to break your neck?" she asked with red eyes.

"No, my dear," he replied calmly.

"Stop calling me your dear. I am not your dear. That dirty, stinking girl of yours is your dear."

Since they got married, they lived happily. They lived in harmony. They were hand in glove. But now they started living like antagonists. He just couldn't find a way to convince her that he didn't know the girl.

All the respect that Mwira had for Grey was gone. Any joke he cracked, she would comment, "What if that dirty, stinking girl of yours heard that joke, wouldn't she enjoy it?" He, therefore, joked no more. Everyone had to mind his or her own business.

It was then that he discovered love is a thing you can put on and off. Mwira loved him at first. He never dreamt they would one day be in such a situation. What fueled the indifference was the fact she came from a family where both parents were short tempered. As a matter of fact, two of her brothers were boxers.

Grey fought tooth and nail to retain Mwira's love but he failed. One morning, he tried to win back her love, "Set your heart at rest, Mwira." She replied, "Just be in my shoes, you'll understand me better."

Now his trust was in the creator. He had no other means of solving this problem. One night the devil whispered to him, "Come on young man, why don't you simply seek a divorce!" That sounded reasonable. What else could he do? Deep down in his heart, he still had burning love for his wife, Mwira. No matter how rude she became, he still respected her. He just didn't want to lose her. She was so beautiful.

"Mwira, we can't continue living like this. This weekend we should go home and end our marriage," he proposed.

"You are quite right. What I want is ashes to ashes, dust to dust," she commented.

Weekend came. They set off for Manda Bus Stage. They took the Nkolokosa bus to Blantyre Bus Stands. Just as they dropped from the bus, Mole who had led to the breakage of their marriage ran after them. The couple saw her. Grey was troubled in his heart. He almost hit her had it not been for the Depot Inspector who came to the rescue. "Hey go away Mole, don't rob people of their peace!" the inspector shouted. When she saw him, she retreated.

"Sir, what's wrong with that girl?" Grey inquired from the inspector.

"Well, don't worry, she is mentally disturbed. She is fond of running after men claiming they are the fathers of her kid," he explained.

With an apprehensive face, Mwira looked at Grey. She hugged him. "Sorry darling, I wronged you. I took things for granted," she apologised and kissed him. Tears rolled down her apple shaped cheeks.

7

THE UGLY SAVIOUR

Msula village had an ugly old woman. She had a bald head, a beard, a flat back and twisted legs. Her lips were deep red and very thick. She had a deep voice like that of a man. Her ears resembled those of a chimpanzee. She had unevenly spaced brown teeth. The odour from her breath stank like rotten meat. She was the right candidate for an ugly contest.

Children mocked her. Songs were composed describing her ugliness. They were sung during festivals. When she heard the songs, she wept. Her eyes were always red and in tears. She regretted having been born. She wished she were as beautiful as the other ladies. But she had no choice. She didn't choose to be born ugly. Her ugliness deprived her of a husband. In her late eighties, she remained single.

Her ugliness was a disgrace to the village. People from other villages flocked to have a glance of her. They gathered around her. They burst out with laughter. When one group left, another group came, so forth and so forth. She had no peace of mind. Her relatives, who were supposed to console her, were the ones fuelling the mockery. Several times she attempted to commit suicide.

One day village Chief, Senda called for a meeting. The agenda for the meeting was the construction of a house in the forest for the ugly old woman. When the agenda was read, people clapped hands in agreement to the proposal. Nobody objected. None of her relatives sympathised with her. The house was constructed and she was dumped in the forest. She had no one to assist her.

The first day that she was dumped, they brought her food to eat. As time went by, nobody bothered to bring her food. The excuse was that the distance was too long. The poor old woman fell in love with starvation. She lived on wild fruits. She searched for them and took them home to eat. The forest had lions, hyenas, leopards, pythons and baboons. Surprisingly, they never harmed her. Leopards slept outside her house. They protected her as dogs would have done.

Fortunately, her house was constructed near Seka River. This river provided her with water to drink and bath. But the problem was, she had no cup and no pail. She used her palm to draw water and drink. She took her bath by dipping herself into the river. She had no soap to use neither for bathing nor washing her clothes. At night when she felt thirsty, leopards escorted her to the river to quench her thirst.

Time went by, food became so scarce. Life became unbearable for Dada, for that was her name. Fearing that she would die of hanger, she set off one day for the village to beg for food. She also needed things like: soap, a pail, a cup and a plate. When people saw her, they released dogs to chase her. Since she was very old, she fell down. The dogs bit her and left her half dead. She was picked in that state and dumped in the forest.

Aida, a little girl who was not her relation, was moved with compassion. One day, she secretly set off for the forest. She brought her food, soap, a plastic pail and medicines. She reached the old woman's house. She handed over the items to her. Dada took out the food and ate.

Aida left for the river to draw her some water. When she returned, she cleaned her wounds and bathed her. Dada was so appreciative. The God given gift spent some time to cheer her up. She got healed psychological and physically.

From that day on, every morning Aida sneaked from the village to bath the old lady. She brought her soya porridge mixed with ground nuts flour. In the afternoon, she brought her cooked rice with beans and in the evening, she brought her rice with chicken. With that, the old woman's health was restored.

The village believed that the old ugly woman was dead. She couldn't have survived with untreated dog bite wounds. One of the dogs that bit her died of rabies. Nobody brought her food to eat. They could not figure it out how an old woman like her could have survived without taking food. Nobody dared to visit her. The fear was, if she had died then the body would have decompose and not good for human sight.

One afternoon when Aida brought her food, she noticed that Dada was in a jovial mood. She was surprised. She thought within herself, "What could have happened for her to be in such a mood?" She came close to her and she smiled, she also smiled back. She hugged her.

"Your face looks bright today, what happened?" she complemented.

"It should, my dear!"

"Why is that so?"

"I have some good news for you."

"What good news?"

"Firstly, let me take this opportunity to thank you very much for your love and care. Without you, I should have been dead by now. You are my saviour. I urge you to continue with your love and care to those in need. My last request is, from now on, stop bringing me some food."

"Why should I stop bringing you some food, have you given up on life or you are you on hunger strike?"

"No, my dear, I have not given up on life; neither am I on hunger strike."

"How are you going to survive without food?"

"There's a huge bird that brings me delicious and nutritious food."

In the course of their discussions, the huge bird landed with a basket. It placed it before Dada. It flew away. It was a very beautiful. It had white feathers on the head, yellow and blue on different parts of her body.

"My dear, what you've seen is what happens here."

"How often does it come?"

"It comes three times a day. It comes in the morning, afternoon and in the evening. It flies away. Immediately I have finished eating, it comes to collect the basket."

Dada took out the food from the basket. Aida was surprise, the basket contained chips, sausages, bananas, bread, stock margarine, a table knife and a bottle of milk. She was invited to eat the food. When she tasted chips, sausages, bananas, bread and milk, she discovered that they had similar tastes to the foods they ate at home. She turned and looked at the old woman. She smiled at her. She also smiled back. The food was so delicious. When they had finished eating, they put back the plates in the basket.

"Please, when you get back home, keep this as a secret."

"I will do exactly what you have instructed me to do."

"Remember, nobody wishes me well in that village. If they discovered my miracle, they would kill me."

"I know, but I forgot to tell you what is at stake at home."

"Tell me before you leave."

"Tiya, the village Chief's son is critically ill. The native doctor who is attending to him has prescribed an orange fruit as the treatment for his illness. Incidentally, our village does not have orange fruits. Our neighbouring villages don't have either. But the boy has got very few hours to live. The village Chief has promised to reward handsomely, whosoever brings and orange fruit. The whole village is shaken."

"Has he disclosed the type of reward for the exercise?"

"Yes, he has."

"What is it?"

"Whosoever brings an orange fruit would be crowned the deputy village Chief."

"Don't worry, you'll become his deputy."

"How will that happen?"

"One of the fruit the huge bird brings me is an orange."

"Wow!"

Sound of a huge bird flying in air was heard. Dada and Aida looked up the sky. They saw it approaching them. Finally, it landed. It delivered oranges. It opened its mouth and sang a very beautiful tune. It picked the basket and flew away. Dada and Aida watched it disappear into the white clouds. They took the oranges and ate. The taste was marvellous.

"The oranges taste so nice," Aida comprehended.

"You are quite right. What I have noticed is that almost all foods brought by this huge bird are delicious."

"I noted that as well. But where does this bird come from?"

"It is very difficult to know because it doesn't talk."

"Try to talk to it one day, it might respond."

"I will. Now take one orange and give it to the village Chief."

"Thank you very much."

Aida bid farewell to the old woman and left. On her way home, she kept asking herself what prompted her to be assisting the abandoned old woman. She couldn't find the answer. She started imagining herself being the deputy Village Chief. "If indeed the medicine worked what will my title be, the deputy village Chief?' she imagined within herself.

When she reached home, she went straight to the village Chief's house. She knocked at the door. He came out. He greeted her:

"Young lady, how are you?"

"I am fine and you, Sir?" she replied.

"I am fine. What can I do for you?"

"I have brought you an orange."

"What? wow! where did you get it from?"

"It's a long story, first hand over the orange to the native doctor and we discuss other issues latter."

"Thank you very much."

Immediately, the village Chief took the orange to the native doctor who upon using it, Tiya, the village Chief's son got healed. He paid off the amount they had agreed. The whole village was shaken.

Aida's name was on everybody's lips.

Songs of praise for Aida were composed and sung. People danced before her. Inquiries were made about where she got the orange. She revealed that the source of the fruit was the ugly old woman. People questioned who that woman was since everybody took it that she had died long time ago.

He called for a meeting. He wanted to crown Aida as his deputy. She sat next to him. She put on a national wear with red and green colours. She had cream regalia on her head. Traditional dances were organised. The common local dance in this village was 'Manganje.'

The mode of dress for 'Manganje' was dried banana leaves. Dried wild fruits were tied around the waist and below both legs. People sang and danced in a circle in clock wise direction. At a certain point they all shouted and all fell down in unison and stood up again quickly. This was done repeatedly. The whole atmosphere was filled with ululation. Soft drinks and a local drink, 'Thobwa,' were served. They had a wonderful time.

"We have all gathered here today to witness the crowning of Aida as the deputy village headman," he started off. Women ululated and clapped hands while men whistled. "My son was almost dead but now he is alive. The person behind all that is none other than, Aida. There is a lesson to learn from this incident: We should stop looking down upon women and the youth. They have a role to play in our society. Our task is to empower them," he wound up his speech. A heavy clap of hands followed.

After the speech, she was crown as the deputy Chief. She was the first woman to become the village headman. She made her own history. Surprisingly, she was not the favourite child in their family. Her parents loved Miriam more than her.

Aida was black in complexion while her sister was brown. Nobody in their family understood what had happened to her but there is nothing they could do. It is wrong for parents to love one child and hate the other. It is the contents that give a bottle a name and not vice versa.

She stood up to offer her acceptance speech. Hand clapping took its turn. As usual, women   ululated. She turned to the village headman. She bent her legs as if to kneel down and stood up. That was how women showed their respect to the elderly and those in authority. She held her palm on her mouth and coughed to clear her throat.

"Let me give thanks to our village Chief for according me such an honour. I am a young girl from a poor family," she started off, "My crowning as a deputy village Chief should act as a lesson to my fellow youth. Most youth of today we act irresponsibly. We don't respect our elders. Let us learn to respect the elders for us to become productive future leaders," Aida addressed the villagers. Clapping of hands, whistling and ululation filled the air.

One thing people wanted to hear from the deputy village Chief was, where and how she got the orange fruit. She started by rebuking the whole village by chasing away the ugly old lady from the village. "I am sure all of you remember Dada the ugly old woman. She was chased out of the village and dumped in the forest to die. I am here to shock you that, it is the same poor ugly woman who gave me the orange that has saved life of the village Chief's son," Aida narrated the shocking story.

All the villagers sighed, "No!" Aida shook off her shoulders. She continued to narrate the story, "After chasing her, I secretly brought her food to eat. I bathed her. In the end she stopped me from bringing her the food. Instead, a huge yellow bird brought her food three times a day."

Everybody was moved by the ugly woman's story. Aida concluded by saying, "Negatives are developed in the darkroom. Each one of us has his or her positive sides. Don't dwell very much on one's negatives. Learn to dwell on one's positives."

The village Chief called off the meeting.

"Aida escort us to the immediately," the village Chief requested.

"What about tomorrow?"

"Why not today.?"

"Because I have to go and inform her first before we set off for the forest."

"If you do that, she wouldn't allow us to visit her. We tortured her and she would think that now we want to kill her. For things to work out nicely, she needs a surprise visit."

"What is the motive of the visit?"

"I want to bring her back to the village. She has to be rewarded for saving the life of my son."

"I very much doubt if she would accept to return to the village."

"Let us give it a try."

They all set off. They all wore sombre faces of regret. They chanted songs of praise for Dada. They clapped hands, whistled and ululated. She heard the songs from a distance. She was frightened. She wanted to run away but something stopped her. Little by little, the sound of songs and footsteps approached her house. "I suppose now they just want to finish me," she thought to herself, "But isn't my ugliness enough, why should they take away my life!" She spoke to herself fearing the worst.

Sound of songs and footsteps increased. The group walked towards her. Before they could get hold of her, a big yellow bird appeared. It lifted her. She smiled and waved bye, bye!

The bird sang a very beautiful song and flew away. The chief and all the villagers were amazed. With mouth wide open, they watched the ugly old woman being whisked away. The bird disappeared into the blue sky.

8

NO SECOND CHANCE

Phata was a student at Guza Government Secondary School. He was short and light - brown in complexion. His mother was a South African but married to a Malawian. He had dimples on both sides of his plump cheeks. He was very handsome. He walked with one shoulder higher than the other. His clothes showed that he came from a wealthy family.

Phata's father was the General Manager for Dish Cash Electrical Engineers. He was tall and brown in complexion. He had a big tummy. He seemed to have everything going for him. He had a posh car and a mansion. He was always smartly dressed.

Pocket money for Phata was equivalent to that of the teachers' salary. Time and gain, he was sent out of class for not wearing a school uniform. He never combed his hair. He was in most cases caught out of bounds. He walked around the school campus with his arms slid in his trousers' pockets. But nevertheless, he was very intelligent.

When schools closed, his father drove to Guza Government Secondary School to pick him up. He brought him sweets and biscuits. He took them as they drove back home. His holidays were wonderful. They ate good meals.

"I understand the food you eat at school is of poor quality?" his mother asked him one school holiday. She pampered him.

"That is true, mum. It is not fit for human consumption but goats," he replied.

When schools opened, he opted to eat at Jean's Tasty Foods Restaurant. It was located at Bazi trading centre. The trading centre was half a kilometre away from the school. But it was compulsory for students to eat at the school cafeteria. He was so scared to eat food from the school cafeteria.

Phata's mother convinced her private doctor to issue exemption medical report for her son to be allowed to take meals outside the campus. That did not go well with the headmaster. He called for him. He went to the headmaster's office. He was ushered into the office by Reza, the school messenger.

"Sit down young man," the headmaster welcomed him.

"Thank you, Sir," he replied as he tucked in his uniform shirt.

"How are you?"

"I am fine, Sir and how are you?"

"I am all right. I called you just to find out if indeed it is true that you take your meals outside the campus?"

"It is true."

"Why do you do that?"

"I am so scared to take meals from the school kitchen."

"You want them to cook the way they cook it at your home?"

"Yes, Sir."

"If that is the case, then collect your luggage and go home, simple."

"That is not what I meant, Sir. I was only registering a concern."

"Without wasting my time, what you have to know is, you came here to learn and not to eat. For your father to become the General Manager, he had to go through all this. The food you enjoy at home is not yours. You have to make your own food. The posh car your father drives is his. It is not yours, so don't be proud for nothing."

Phata realised that the headmaster had lost his temper. He apologised, "I am sorry, Sir."

"If you are sorry, stop taking food at the trading centre, is that clear?"

"It is clear, Sir."

In the evening, he sneaked from school. . He went to the trading centre to eat and enjoy himself. Without the knowledge of his father, his mother sent him money for the meals. Availability of money, prompted him to start drinking beer. While his friends were studying, he was busy chasing prostitutes in pubs.

Though he was young, prostitutes loved him so much. He had what they were looking for, money. Apart from the money issue, he was handsome. The hooligans nicknamed him, "Whiteman." When he entered the pubs, they all shouted, "The white man is in!" He spent his time enjoying himself. He had no time to copy notes or study. He hired his fellow students to copy notes for him and paid them. His friends nick named him, "General Manager."

Students with bad character admired the way he conducted himself. But those with good character pitied him. On Wednesdays, students were allowed to wear casual clothes. But Mphata dressed formally, decent clothes and shoes. He looked like a member of staff. Visitors mistook him for a teacher.

Time flies. Examination time approached. Phata was cornered. He had spent his time fooling around. He never took his studies seriously. In English Literature subject, they had three books on the syllabus. He had read only one. They had to read three textbooks for History. He had read none. His class - teacher, Thuza had been warning him but he did not take the advice.

"You will be writing your exams shortly, make use of the remaining period. I wish you all the best. I've all the hope that all of you will do well," Thuza encouraged the students. "Excuse me, Sir, I do not understand topic four in our Geography workbook," Phata interrupted. The whole class booed him.

"That's the topic I spent more time on. If you never concentrated when I taught, I am afraid, there is nothing I can do now," Thuza replied.

Phata was fond of asking obvious questions. His main aim was to confuse the teachers. Teachers bore with him. They knew he was proud. Teaching was stopped. Students were given free time to study on their own and hold discussions on different topics. He took his history notes to study. He discovered that he had forgotten almost everything. He took one literature book to read. He understood nothing.

"Chada, I propose we study in the forest to avoid disturbances," Phata suggested to his best friend.

"I totally agree with you," he replied.

Chada, Phata's friend; came from a poor family. Their association changed his status. He dressed up like a child from a well to do family. He borrowed his friend's clothes and wore them. Since his friend had nice clothes, it made his poverty invisible.

Chada's father was a watch man at Chinangwa Milling Company. He had a very low income. Payment of school fees for his son was a hassle. The company he worked for was owned by an Indian. He was fairly old. He enjoyed uttering obscene vernacular expressions. After uttering them, he burst out with heavy laughter that ended in a heavy cough. He wasn't very particular about where to spit when the laughter was over.

Phata and Chada started moving together in form four. They enjoyed booze and smoking. Both of them were doing well before they came together. Teachers had trust in them that they would make it for the university. The moment they started moving together, their performance went down.

In an attempt to try and catch up with time, they studied in the forest. When fellow students discovered it, they advised them to stop since the area was a home of deadly snakes. They didn't heed to the advice. They thought it was mere jealousy. The school prefect reported the matter to the class teacher. He feared they would be stung by the deadly snakes.

Thuza called them, "I hear you study in that forest. Please, stop it. Anything can happen there and we'll be answerable." They both replied,

"We'll stop it, Sir."

At the hostel, Phata threatened, "Who reported to Thuza that we study in the forest?"

"I did," Phoso, the prefect replied. Phata almost hit him. Chada rebuked his friend.

"We will continue to study in the forest. Anyone who'll report us to Thuza will feel it thick. We go there because the place is conducive for studies and please put your hands off our business," Phata sounded a warning. They indeed continued to study in the forest.

Phoso, the prefect was a lovely boy. He couldn't stand it, to leave Phata and Chada risk their lives by continuing to study in the forest. He, therefore, reported the matter again to Thuza. "Leave them to do what they want," he replied. After that, nobody stopped them from going into the forest. They were always in the forest. Whenever they came back for lunch, they boasted, "Malaya University Boys."

"Comrade, what are you going to study at Malaya University?" Phata asked his friend at the top of his voice in the Dinning - Hall.

"Public Administration," he replied.

"And you?"

"Education," Phata replied, "I'll come and teach here. Thuza and I will be fellow members of staff," he continued boasting.

Phata showed off when girls were around. He bragged at the top of his voice about going abroad with his dad after the examinations. He switched from one girl friend to another. The shocking thing about most girls at this school was that, they loved troublesome boys. He had more than one girlfriend. He was the talk of the school. In his pair of jeans trousers, he walked around the school compound pompously like a member of staff.

"Chada, what are your plans when we are done with secondary education?" Phata inquire from his friend one afternoon.

"I will go home and prepare gardens in preparation for the next season's planting season."

"Don't you have workers?"

"No, we don't have."

"So you mean to say that your parents use you as their worker?"

"Yes."

"Are workers scarce at your home?"

"No."

"You have to advise your parents to employ at least four workers?"

"My father cannot afford."

"Why?"

"He receives a very low salary."

"What is his profession?"

"He is a watch man. In your case, you are very lucky. Your father is a General Manager."

Studying in the forest continued. Back from there, the duo sang what they had memorised. They disturbed other student's peace in the hostel. They knew they had been studying and even if they made some noise, they wouldn't lose anything. The school prefect tried to stop them. Phata blasted him.

"Shut up! close your pit latrine," he shouted.

"What do you mean?" the prefect asked angrily.

"What I mean is, your mouth is no better than a pit latrine," he repeated his rude remarks.

"So my mouth is a pit latrine?"

"Yes, what else do you think it is?"

"If that is the case, yours is a placenta pit."

Phata lost his temper. He closed in to the school prefect but before he could hit him, Ulemu, a giant student at the school intervened. He warned, "Should you dare beat him up, I will deal with you. I will squeeze you like a sponge. Why are you so proud? Is it because of your father's wealth? You should work hard and earn it for yourself." Immediately, he shied away.

A day to the exams, Phata and his friend left for final preparations. "Chada, today we should not be in one place. I'm going to be a few metres away from you but where we can see each other if at all there is anything to discuss," he explained. He left. Whenever they had something to discuss, they did so. Chada had something to share with his friend. He called him but got no response. He went to check on him. He was terrified. A big snake calmly lay on his friends back. It caught flies.

"My God!" he sighed, "So my friend has been killed by a deadly snake. I'll not disturb it. I'll rush to report," Chada thought within himself as he trembled.

He rushed back to school. He went firstly to the prefect.

"Phata has been killed by a snake," he reported. Both Chada and the prefect reported the issue to Thuza, "Phata has been killed by a snake." Thuza replied sorrowfully, "Can you see now Chada? We stopped you from studying in the forest just to save your lives."

Thuza reported the matter to the headmaster, Duncan. He instructed them and other students to go and collect the body. When girls heard the sad story, they wept. The school was in a very confused state. All the students wore somber faces.

All discussions were in whispers. Chada directed the rescue team to the spot where his friend's body lay. He warned them not to make noise. They moved quietly. As they approached the body, they found the snake enjoying its time on the victim's back.

They all decided to kill the snake right there on his back, fearing it could escape. Chada took a steel water pipe which he brought from school. He raised it in the air and brought down at Phata's back. He missed it and hit his right hand.

Phata woke up. He screamed, "My hand, my hand, my hand!" The snake ran away. The hand was crashed to pieces. He fainted. Everybody sighed, "So he wasn't dead!" It was a sad moment. He wasn't dead as they thought. He was asleep. The snake never bit him. It had only found a nice and comfortable place to rest.

Phata was rushed to the hospital. He was bleeding heavily. He was admitted. His right hand was amputated. After an hour, he opened his eyes. He saw Thuza, Chada and other students around his bed. He frowned. He coughed continuously for three seconds.

"Where am I?" he inquired.

"In hospital," Thuza replied.

"What am I doing here?"

"You have been admitted."

"Admitted at which hospital?"

"You have been admitted at Chikowi Government Hospital."

"Admitted on what grounds?"

"You have been involved in an accident."

By then, he was not aware that his hand had been amputated. Pain killers were busy killing the pain. It was difficult for Thuza to reveal to him that he had lost one hand. He turned and looked at Chada.

"How is it going, my dear friend? he asked smiling.

"It is going on very well," Chada replied sorrowfully.

Phata closed his eyes. He went into coma once more. A heavy snoring sound filled the whole side ward. The following morning, examinations began. He was absent. He was in hospital. He was in a state of confusion. He was in his own world.

Phata lost memory.

"How are you, Sir?" the doctor greeted him.

"I am fine," he replied.

'If you are fine, what are you doing here?" the doctor joked.

"That is the question I should pose to you," he replied.

The doctor smiled.

"By the way, what is the date today?" the doctor asked.

He comfortably mention the previous year. He was living in the past. He knew not what was happening. The examinations ended without him knowing anything.

After two months, Phata was discharged from hospital. He now had one hand, the left hand. He had the task of learning to write using the remaining hand. Initially, he was right handed but the tragedy left him with one left hand. Malawi School Certificate of Education results were out. Chada his good friend scored good points. He was selected for university studies.

The tragedy left Phata with one option, to repeat. He was offered a place to repeat in form four. This time he had good character. He had leant a bitter lesson. He was ready to learn. He had great respect for teachers as well as his fellow students. Girls who used to flock for him never did so again. The association had been broken. He had one hand.

Teachers were his consolation. Weekend lessons were organised specifically for him. Other students also benefited from that facility. He became the teachers' favourite. They were very willing to help him. "Phata, if you had taken my advice into account, by now you could have been in the university. But it's never too late, work hard. You'll make it." Thuza consoled him.

One weekend, Phata's parents decided to pay him a visit. They brought him groceries. But they forgot to bring him his favourite stuff: Cornflakes. They promised to bring him during the next visit. They were very happy to learn that he was a changed boy. His character had changed for the better. It made them more proud to learn that he was the school prefect.

In the afternoon, Phata's father and mother bid him farewell. They both hugged and kissed him. Finally, they blessed him. They jumped into their posh car. He waved at them. They waved back. The car sped off. He picked a white plastic bag that contained groceries. He took it and left it at the hostel.

Phata's fellow students who came from poor families admired the plastic bag. Gobo, one of the students couldn't help begging, "Can you give me that plastic bag so that I can be put in my clothes." He smiled and handed it over to him. "Thank you very much," Gobo expressed his gratitude.

Phata started off for the classroom to study. On the way he saw Thuza running towards him helplessly. They met. He held him by the hand and took him to the staff room. His heart started beating fast. He thought to himself, "What crime have I committed?" The headmaster sat on his arm chair. Trace of tears could be seen in his eyes.

"Good afternoon, Phata," the headmaster greeted.

"Good afternoon, Sir."

The headmaster looked up the ceiling. He turned to Thuza. He glanced at him. Thereafter, he turned to Phata.

"We have very bad news for you," the headmaster began, "Your parents have been involved in a fatal car accident. Both of them have died on the spot."

Phata fell off from his chair. He collapsed. Thuza and the headmaster administered First Aid on him. He opened his eyes. He groaned, "No second chance!"

9

CRAZY MINIBUS DRIVER

The minibus was cruising dangerously. Wind blew so strongly through a broken glass that made life very uncomfortable for the passengers. The alarm which signaled a need for speed reduction was ringing. With his hair uncombed, Jola; the driver ignored it. Music was playing very loudly through the minibus' speakers.

"Mum, have you noted that all trees are moving backwards in the opposite direction," Bola, a little boy who sat on her mother's lap expressed his concern.

"My son, those trees are not moving," her mother replied with a smiled.

"Then what's happening?" Bola asked as he shrugged his shoulders.

"That is what happens when a car is moving," Mala, the little boy's mother explained.

"My fear is, by the time we reach home; we won't find trees," Bola raised his concern. All the passengers burst out with laughter.

The minibus driver never reduced speed. He held the steering with one hand. He shook his head in response to the music that was on full blast. He sung along the music that was coming out of the speakers. He overtook every vehicle that was ahead of him.

"Hey driver, can you slow down?" An elderly man with grey hair requested politely. The driver just glanced backwards. He did not reply neither did he slow down. Instead he fixed his cap and increased the speed. He looked back a second time. He smiled as though everything was fine.

"What is your name, Sir?" he asked the elderly man with grey hair.

"My name is Jamu."

"Why are you so afraid, do you want to clock hundred years?"

Before Jamu could answer back, Jola saw a prospective passenger stopping the minibus. He slowed down. He switched on the left indicator. He stopped at the stage. The conductor opened the door. The passenger came in.

The passenger was wearing sun hat. He looked drunk. A lady passenger was ordered to shift to the left to give room to the new passenger. She shifted. The door was closed. The minibus took off. A smell of 'Kachasu', a local gin beer filled the whole minibus.

"Mr. Conductor, my name is Dazi Langa," the drunkard passenger introduced himself.

"So what?" the conductor replied rudely.

"I have three questions for you, Sir."

"Go ahead, ask."

"The first question is, 'Is your mother a man or a woman?'"

"Sir, don't silly."

"Never mind, the second question is, 'When did you last take a bath?'"

"Sir, I have warned you already not to be silly."

"The last question is, 'When did you last brush your teeth?'"

"That's none of your business."

"It is my business. I am feeling very uncomfortable in here. You just can't wake up without taking bath! The odour from your armpits and mouth, is terrible. It stinks like a rotten dog," the drunkard passenger expressed himself boldly as he stammered.

The whole minibus burst out with laughter. The conductor was upset. "He shouted, "What's funny?" Nobody replied. There was a cathedral silence. The driver was ordered to stop. He slowed down and stopped. The passengers' door was slid.

The drunkard passenger was pushed out. He staggered and fell down. He stood up and sucked his saliva. He remarked, "I will never board your stinking minibus again." The door was closed. The journey continued.

"Driver, you wondered why I feared for my life?" Jamu resumed their discussions.

"Yes, Sir, you are probably the oldest person in here, yet you are so afraid of death."

"You are quite right; I am a responsible family man."

"What has that got to do with me?"

"Your task is to transport us and not to kill us."

"Old man, what am I doing in here; am I not transporting you?"

"I told you that my name is Jamu and not old man."

"Forgive me, but are you not old?"

"Shut up! what are you up to?"

"I am up to nothing, Sir."

"Do you enjoy quarrelling with passengers?"

"No, Sir, what you have to know is that, those who are meant to die today can not die tomorrow."

Like a swarm of bees, everybody in the minibus hummed. Monica, the youngest lady in the minibus chipped in, "Frustrated drivers are always very careless on the road. All they want is to commit suicide." That statement irked Jola. He stepped on the brake. The minibus stopped.

"Lady, get out!" he shouted angrily.

"Nooo!" booed the other passengers in unison.

"No! what do you mean? Is this your minibus? You poverty stricken people!" he shouted. The whole minibus was quiet. He got off his seat. He opened the passengers' door. He grabbed the lady and pulled her out. He slapped her and closed the door. He went back to his seat and started off again. The minibus was quiet.

"My son, you would make a good boxer than a minibus driver," Jamu commented boldly.

Jola turned back. He was annoyed by the statement. He sucked his saliva. He spotted a pothole on the tarmac road. Deliberately, he never dodged it. Passengers flew from their sets. They hit the ceiling of the minibus. They all sighed, "Gosh!" The minibus swerved. He managed to control it.

"Am I your son, did you give birth to me?" he asked with rage showing on his face.

"No."

"Can you give birth to a handsome son like me?"

Jamu burst out with laughter. He asked, "Who cheated you that you are handsome?"

"I know it myself."

"I am sorry my son, you are not handsome. Your face is no better than that of a hippopotamus."

"I told you already that I am not your son."

"You are quite right, you can't be my son. My handsome son has good manners."

"I can take the day light out of you," the driver threatened.

"You, as young as you are, take the day light out of me? You are joking. I pity your parents. They didn't finish their assignment on you."

"What assignment?"

"You were poorly brought up. You are a disgrace. You are irresponsible. You are a savage."

Jola lost his temper. He stopped the minibus. He switched off the engine. Before he came out, Jamu quickly jumped off and ran away. "You are a fool!" he shouted at the top of his voice. Jamu replied, "You are an idiot!" He switched on the engine and left.

As he sped, a bee found its way into the minibus. Experience has shown that when such a thing happens, it doesn't matter whom you are sitting next to, whether your wife or child, you just brush it off to the person next to you before you are stung.

The bee landed on the first passenger. He brushed it off to his neighbour. While the minibus was still cruising, the second person brushed it off to Jola. It stung him. "Ooow!" he was screamed. The minibus swerved off the road. It hit a baobab tree. There was a loud bang. Bodies flew in the air and on the ground. Human limbs were splattered against the baobab tree.

Streams of blood flowed. Some dead bodies had eyes wide open as if regretting why they never dropped off on the way. Others had eyes closed as if in deep sleep but with no scratch on them. All passengers who remained in the minibus passed on.

Jola was the only survivor. He had compound fractures on both legs. He was bleeding from his nose. He was unconscious. When he awakened, he realised that he was on a hospital bed. Both legs were amputated. Doctors had not revealed to him about the amputation, neither did he notice it.

Kabila, a fellow minibus driver heard about the incident. He was moved with compassion. He inquired the hospital he was admitted to. He visited him. He had heard about the amputation of the two legs. He couldn't imagine a minibus driver without legs. He was touched.

"Sorry for the loss of your two legs," Kabila consoled Jola.

"You are talking about loss of two legs, which legs?" Jola asked confused. Kabila realised that he had made a blunder for the owner had not been informed about the amputation. He decided to change the topic.

"By the way, what happened?"

"What happened where?"

"I mean for the accident to take place."

Kabila was at pains to break the sad news. He pretended he had received a phone call. He removed the cell phone from its casing. He placed it on his left ear and walked out of the ward. He murmured to himself, "I have made a blunder, Jola is not aware of the amputation and what can I do now?" He returned to the ward.

"Friend, I have to rush for an emergency hire," he cheated.

"Okay, all the best, thank you for visiting me."

Kabila left. Immediately, Jola slid his hands between the two bed sheets. He couldn't feel his legs. All he could feel were bandages. He pushed the hands further. Legs were nowhere to be felt. Pools of tears ran down his skinny cheeks. He murmured to himself, "So this is what Kabila meant! " He stared at the ceiling. He saw a lizard. It was chasing a cockroach. He murmured once more, "I am now disabled. What a life!"

10

THE GRANDSON

Evening came. Chiko was in the sitting room. He was listening to the radio. His mother, Leya was inside her grass - thatched kitchen. It had poor ventilation. Thick soot hung from the roof. A paraffin lamp hung from a wire that was suspended from the roof. She was baking scones for the following morning sales.

"Mum, it's going to rain soon!" he warned.

"Let it rain. I have to complete my job otherwise we'll have no relish tomorrow," she replied.

The sky was as dark as a dark room. Dark and thick rain clouds sped in the sky. One could not see the stars. They were buried in the clouds. Lightening flashed and thunder roared. Not long, rain drops began to fall and then a downpour. Chiko ran back into the kitchen. It was leaking heavily.

"Mum, let us go inside the house," he pleaded with her.

"Go, I'll find you there," she answered.

He ran back into the house. He felt sorry for her. Their thatched house was also leaking heavily. He thought to himself, "Where is my father? Why are we suffering like this?" Chiko had no father. He grew up with a single parent. Each time he tried to inquire about his father's whereabouts, he got no concrete answer. His mother dropped off from school. She took care of all the house chores. They survived on scone business.

"Chiko!" his mother called. He ran into the kitchen.

"I am through so help me to collect the pots and what have you into the house," They collected everything and ran back into the house. Her clothes were soaked as I she fell in the rain.

She prepared supper. They ate. The whole roof leaked except Chiko's bedroom. They had tough time. His mother fought tooth and nail to stop the leak but to no avail. She had just finished baking the scones. She needed time to rest. The situation never granted her that rest.

Chiko started dozing. She, therefore, made his bed for him to sleep. He slept. She continued to struggle with the leak. In the morning Chiko took a bath. After the bath, he took his breakfast. He packed his books in his school bag ready to go.

"Chiko, my son, work hard at school so that you become a productive citizen in future. He smile and replied, "Be assured that I will try my best to work hard. I will bail you out of poverty.

After school, Chiko took over the scone business from his mother. She sold the scones at a Lanje Mission Hospital. He wondered why she sold them there yet there was a secondary school nearby.

"Mum, why don't you sell the scones at Mangunde Secondary School?"

"Students are very troublesome. I used to sell them there in the past but I ended up coming back with nothing."

"What happened?"

"They approached me in a group as if to buy the scones, but while there; one would shout, "A snake!" I ran away leaving the scone basket behind. They picked the scones and disappeared."

"Did you see the snake?"

"No, it was false. All they wanted was to scare me so that I ran away and they steal the scones. But as for you, don't worry, go and sell them there. Students love kids. They won't steal from you," she advised.

Chiko sold the scones at Mangunde Secondary School. Most students loved him. Some of them invited him to their hostels. They assisted him with his assignments. Others called for clothes from their young brothers and offered him.

One sunny afternoon, he sat on a grey rock at Mangunde School Market. He sold scones. A man in his forties approached him. He smiled. He bought two scones. As he ate, he sternly stared at Chiko. He wondered what crime he had committed.

"My name is Mphonda. I am the English teacher at Mangunde Secondary School and you?" he introduced himself.

"I am Chiko."

"Are you related to Mr. Phazi, the headmaster?" Mphonda asked.

"No, but Phazi is my surname," he replied.

"You resemble him so much, just hold on; I will be back in a moment." He left. He came back with a slim, tall brown and handsome gentleman. Chiko looked at him admiringly.

"Sir, do you know this boy?" Mphonda asked the headmaster. He looked squarely him.

"No, I don't know him. Don't forget that I am only three months old here. "

"Why I brought you here is because he resembles you. You have a black spot just above your nose and him too," he explained.

"You are quite right, but I don't understand where the resemblance comes from," the headmaster replied as he took a photo of the little boy.

Mphonda and the headmaster returned to school. At home, the headmaster took out a photo of his late son. He compared it with the little boy's photo. The two looked like identical twins. His wife saw him viewing the photos. She was surprised.

"What are you up to?" Sela his wife asked.

"I met a little boy who resembles me and Sato our late son."

"Where was that?"

"I met him at the school market. Infact, it was Mphonda who noticed the resemblance and took me to see for myself."

"Do you have his photograph?"

"Yes, that's what I was looking at. I was comparing late Sato's photo and that of the boy."

"Can I have a look at them?"

"Here you are."

Phazi handed over the photos to his wife, Sela. She sighed, "Wow! they look like identical twins."

"That was my observation as well."

"What was the boy doing at the market?"

"He was selling scones."

"That reminds me something, Sato on his death bed, had something to say that I was unable to grasp. It could have been what we are experiencing now. Anyway just follow it up tomorrow."

The headmaster, Phazi just got transferred from Dovu Secondary School in the Central Region to Mangunde Secondary School in the Southern Region. He was hardly three month old at this school. It was almost twelve years since his son died.

In the afternoon, he visited the school market. He met the boy. He decided to interrogate him.

"What's your name?" the headmaster began the interrogation.

"My name is Sato Phazi."

Phazi, the headmaster was shocked. His late son's name was Sato and the little boy's name was Sato. He scratched his head. He raised his hands and yawned. "What could have happened?" he thought to himself. He scratched his chin that had grey beard.

"Who gave you that name?" he continued the interrogation.

"I was given the name by my dear mum."

"Where is she?"

"She is at home."

"What is the name of your village?"

"The name of my village is Dulira."

"What does she do for a living?"

"She is a business lady."

"What type of business does she do?"

"She sells scones."

"I see. Where is your father?"

"I don't have a father."

"What happened for you to be fatherless?"

"I don't know, each time I try to find out from my mum, she weeps and when that happens, I change the topic."

"How old are you?"

"I am ten years old."

"Do you go to school?"

"Yes, I do."

"In what class are you?"

"I am in standard five."

"At which school are you?"

"I am at Mpondasi Full Primary School."

The headmaster opened the zip for his brown briefcase. He searched for his son's photo. He found it. He closed the briefcase. He handed it over to the little boy. The boy stared at it. He raised his head. Their eyes met. He smiled.

"Why do you smile?" the headmaster inquired.

"You resemble the young man on the photograph," Sato replied.

"Other than that, what else have you noted?"

"I have noted that I also resemble him."

"Okay, follow me," he invited the boy.

Sato lifted the bucket of scones. He followed the headmaster. On the way they met a lady member of staff, Miss Mwale. She stared at the little boy. She asked, "Is he your grandson?" The headmaster replied smilingly, "That is what I want to find out."

At last, the headmaster stood at the front door of his beautiful house. He knocked and opened it. He ushered the little boy in. He called his wife, "Jane!" She ran into the sitting room. Immediately she saw the little boy, she yelped, "Sato, my son!" she hugged him. The little boy was perplexed, "How come she knows my name?" he asked himself.

Jane had six miscarriages in her life. The only child who survived

114

was Sato. He died prematurely at the age of twenty. He was in his third year at Makulawe Polytechnic. He was studying for a degree in civil engineering. He died in his sleep. He never fell sick.

Post - mortem revealed that Sato was choked by saliva. He was a very brilliant boy. A night to his death, he kept asking his friends about what happens after dead. Unfortunately, none of them had experienced death so they had no answer.

"Wow! how are you?" Jane greeted the little boy.

"I am fine thanks and how are you?"

"I am fine."

"What's your name?"

"My name is Sato Phazi."

Jane's heart missed a beat. She was shocked. She turned to her husband as she tightened the cloth she had wrapped on top of her green skirt. She looked squarely onto the little boy's eyes.

"What's happening?" she asked inquisitively.

"That is why I brought this little boy here. Don't bother asking him any more questions. We should allow him to return and bring his mother."

"I would buy your suggestion."

Sato was sent back to his mother. In no time, the two arrived. She had an old umbrella in her hands since it was rainy season. She was poorly dressed.   They were invited into the house. Sato sat on the western side of the sitting room while her mother sat on the northern side. They were served with soft drinks. The little boy's mother kept staring at the headmaster.

"Why do you stare at me like that?" the headmaster asked Sato's mother.

"I am staring at you because you resemble my son," she replied with a wide smile.

"That is why you are here. You have to explain why I resemble your son."

"You also have to explain to me why you resemble my son's dad."

"Who is the father to your son?"

"It's a long story. Bear with me. I was in form one at Dzanza Girls Secondary School. During one school holiday, one Makulawe Polytechnic student by the name of Thope brought a fellow polytechnic student for a holiday. The students name was Sato Phazi. This student met me at the well. He proposed me but I refused. He insisted that he loved me. Realising that I wouldn't yield to his wish, he over powered me. He dragged me into the bush. He raped me."

"Alas!" both the headmaster and his wife sighed.

"I conceived," Leya continued to narrate her ordeal, "My parents were so bitter with me. They never believed that I was raped. They didn't allow me to give my side of the story. They, therefore, disowned me. They kicked me out of their house. I relocated to my grandmother's home, Ndecha."

"We are very sorry about what happened to you. I propose that you return and leave your son with us. We want to take him for a DNA test, should that test prove positive, we will take both of you on board and support you in anyway possible for the rest of your lives."

"Thank you so much, Sir."

Phazi suggested that they go for a group photograph. He invited their neighbour, Pensulo to take the photographs. Four photographs were taken at the sitting room. They all came out and had three photographs at the veranda. Finally, two were taken at a small round about that had very beautiful flowers.

Leya left for her home. The following morning, Sato was taken to Kings Central Hospital for DNA test. The results were positive. He was indeed the headmaster's grandson.

Printed in Great Britain
by Amazon

41403891R00069